Love is
a time of enchantment:
in it all days are fair and all fields
green. Youth is blest by it,
old age made benign:
the eyes of love see
roses blooming in December,
and sunshine through rain. Verily
is the time of true-love
a time of enchantment — and
Oh! how eager is woman
to be bewitched!

GOLDSMITHS' ROW

London 1589. Joel Downes is sent by his former master's widow to look for the grandchild she has never seen. Apparently, Frances Tabor has vanished into thin air, but Joel discovers Grace Wilton, a penniless orphan, who is very pretty and amenable. Joel needs money, he also has a bitter grudge against the Tabor family — why shouldn't he pass off Grace as the missing heiress? However, Joel is not quite as clever as he thinks, while poor Grace is not cut out to be a conspirator.

Books by Sheila Bishop
in the Ulverscroft Large Print Series:

A SPEAKING LIKENESS
THE WILDERNESS WALK
THE PARSON'S DAUGHTER
THE SECOND HUSBAND
THE FAVOURITE SISTER
THE PHANTOM GARDEN
THE DURABLE FIRE

SHEILA BISHOP

GOLDSMITHS' ROW

Complete and Unabridged

ULVERSCROFT
Leicester

First published in Great Britain

First Large Print Edition
published June 1994

British Library CIP Data

Bishop, Sheila
Goldsmiths' Row.—Large print ed.—
Ulverscroft large print series: romance
I. Title
823.914 [F]

ISBN 0–7089–3089–1

Published by
F. A. Thorpe (Publishing) Ltd.
Anstey, Leicestershire

Set by Words & Graphics Ltd.
Anstey, Leicestershire
Printed and bound in Great Britain by
T. J. Press (Padstow) Ltd., Padstow, Cornwall

This book is printed on acid-free paper

1

THERE were ten houses altogether, in an unbroken line. Four storeys high, peaked and gabled, they dominated Cheapside. At ground level their shops opened directly on to the street; above the shops, stretching along the entire façade, were the arms of the Goldsmiths' Company supported by a procession of figures riding monstrous beasts, all cast in lead and covered with gold leaf. The houses were nearly a hundred years old, but the gold images were kept in good repair, and they had a startling magnificence on a bright, uncomfortably cold morning in January, 1589, as they towered over the sleepily stirring market and the muffled group of people with pails and jugs who were trying to break the ice on the water-conduit.

Joel Downes, hurrying into Cheapside from Gutter Lane, saw the familiar skyline without any feeling of elation.

He had a room in Bachelors' Alley, a narrow slit of a back street where young, unmarried journeymen of the Goldsmiths' Company were entitled to a cheap lodging. The bachelors had been celebrating something the night before; he couldn't remember precisely what, only that he had a thick head and he was going to be late at the shop. He could see that all the houses in the Row had their doors open and their shutters thrown back, ready for another day's trade.

All the houses except one. The third door along from the Friday Street end was still firmly closed, and the shutters were fastened across the windows, looking, thought Joel with a horrid aptness, like pennies on a dead man's eyes. He came to a halt, staring at the house where he had spent all his working life.

Another half-awake journeyman bumped into him from behind.

"If you've nothing to do but stand there like an ox in a pond . . . "

"Look, Simon. The shutters are drawn on Tabor's windows. The old man's gone at last."

"Your master? He must have died in

the night. Did you know he was so near the end?"

"He's been sinking these last three days. Even so," said Joel, "I was afraid he meant to live for ever."

"Better guard your tongue. Once he's dead, you are supposed to forget his shortcomings and show a proper respect."

Simon had tweaked off his cap. After a moment's reflection Joel did the same. Then he crossed the road and rapped on the closed door.

"Who's there?" He recognised the voice.

"Let me in, Father."

Zachary Downes dragged back the bolts and opened the door just wide enough to let his son pass through.

"Three o'clock this morning," he said, answering the question Joel had not yet asked. "He never came out of his slumber, my poor old friend. I have to stay near the door, for the neighbours keep coming to enquire; the Astons and the Partridges have been already, and I dare say the Lord Mayor himself will send, as soon as he hears the news."

"Well, he can hardly avoid hearing it much longer."

Sir Richard Martin, the reigning Lord Mayor of London, was a fellow goldsmith and another neighbour, he lived three houses further along the Row.

Zachary Downes clicked his tongue at his son's levity. He was a thin, grey, worried man, not at all like Joel, who was large and blunt-featured and cocksure, with a keen eye to the main chance. Though they did not appear to have much in common, Joel was a surprisingly good son. His affection for his father was almost protective; he considered that Zachary had taken too many hard knocks from life, not least from his dear friend who was lying dead upstairs, and who in life had worked him to the bone, despised, coerced and possibly swindled him. Had John Tabor kept his promise in the end? That remained to be seen.

As they stood in the darkened shop, a girl carrying a silver porringer came through from the kitchen quarters at the back: Philadelphia Whitethorn, Mrs. Tabor's waiting-woman.

"I'm going upstairs, Mr. Downes. Is

4

there anything I can do for you?"

"Not at present, I thank you. I hope you'll find your mistress more comfortable in her mind."

"Her sister is still with her," said Philadelphia obliquely.

Zachary shuffled his feet. "It was right that she should be here. I was obliged to let Edmund fetch his mother; what else could I do?"

"You had no choice. But I think Mrs. Tabor might be thankful if I disturbed her with this sustaining posset."

"What an enterprising creature you are, Del," exclaimed Joel.

The girl smiled faintly. She was tall but very light on her feet with a well-shaped body: widely sprung breasts and a small elegant waist. Her hair was smooth under a little cap of embroidered linen. Her eyes, in this half-light, seemed unusually dark and lustrous.

She passed through the shop, and Joel held aside a curtain for her, so that she could go upstairs into the private part of the house.

The parlour and great chamber were on the first floor, Philadelphia went on up the second flight. There was a staircase window where the curtains had been parted to let in some light. As she came into the shaft of brightness, she raised her hand in a slight brushing movement, as though to ward off the sun. She acted quite unconsciously; there was no one there to see what that futile gesture was trying unsuccessfully to hide; the puckered seam which ran down from the left temple to the bridge of her nose. The forehead that should have been as clear as alabaster was indelibly pitted with the scars of smallpox.

On the second landing Philadelphia paused. Inside the principal bed-chamber John Tabor's body was laid out in his shroud, as she had seen it an hour ago, the muscles of the face slackened and the flesh dropping away, so that the sharp spar of the profile stood out in relief like the prow of a ship. Some men appeared to change character after death; not John Tabor. He had been a tyrant while he lived, and his corpse was stiffening into the mould he had made for himself. She had spent eight months in his house and she had not liked him; no amount of pious meditation was going to alter that.

There was another door, and beyond it she could hear the murmur of women's voices. She hesitated, with the porringer cooling rapidly in her hands. It seemed a fearful impertinence, to break in on the newly-made widow's private conversation with her sister, yet Philadelphia could not help feeling that this was what Mrs. Tabor would probably want her to do.

Alice Tabor and Hannah Beck were the surviving children and co-heiresses of a former Master of the Goldsmiths' Company, Sir Peter Middleton. Alice had married into the same livery, so to speak; Hannah, who was several years younger, had married a mercer, Arthur Beck, with his fine house on London Bridge, had been an excellent match. The Tabors were undoubtedly richer than the Becks, but the Becks were rich enough not to suffer by comparison, and in every other way Hannah had done better than her sister. Alice had been saddled with a most difficult husband; Hannah's husband was meek and devoted and fully aware of his luck in having such an excellent wife. The Tabors' only child, a girl, had died unmarried at the age of eighteen; this must have been a bitter disappointment, and even now, fifteen years later, Philadelphia had never heard either of them speak of her. The Becks, on the other hand, had four sons and four daughters, all of them so healthy, handsome, prudent, diligent and obedient that it was hardly possible to believe they were mortal flesh and blood.

One of the voices behind the door was raised with a sudden squawk of indignation. Philadelphia took a firm grip on the porringer and marched in without knocking.

" . . . Never heard of such an outrageous scheme! My poor Alice, you are overwhelmed by your bereavement. You must forget all these troublesome matters and leave well alone. You'll do no good by trying to dig up the past."

Mrs. Beck was a massive woman with hair the colour of brass, much taller than her woolly, timid sister. The widow wore an old black dress which would tide her over until her brother-in-law had produced all the necessary cloth and velvet for her mourning. She looked flustered, and her weak, rather pleasant face wore an expression of tremulous obstinacy. Thirty-five years of submission to John Tabor had left her without much courage in an argument.

Mrs. Beck spoke irritably to Philadelphia. "We don't require you here at present, my good girl. Your mistress will send for you when you are needed."

"But I am very glad to see Philadelphia," said Mrs. Tabor. "I want to tell her of my plan. What do you think I am going to do, my dear? I am going to send for my grand-daughter and bring her here to live with me.

Philadelphia gazed at her in astonishment. She did not know that Mrs. Tabor had a grand-daughter.

2

"IT was news to me," protested Philadelphia to Joel Downes, late that afternoon, when they were toasting their feet in front of the furnace in the workshop. The shop itself was still shut, of course, though a certain activity of lights and voices was stealing through a crack in the door. Edmund Beck had the two apprentices in there — Will Morris and Joel's younger brother Sam — they were polishing the plate, which soon tarnished in the foggy London air and needed constant attention. It was like Edmund to think of doing this at such a time; he was Mrs. Beck's youngest son and exceedingly conscientious. Joel, a far more accomplished craftsman, saw no point in making work for himself, and was perfectly at ease gossiping with Philadelphia.

"Did you know there was a grand-child?" she asked him.

"Yes, but I always supposed it had

perished in infancy."

"But who were the parents? Had Mr. and Mrs. Tabor any other family except that girl — what was her name? Frances?"

"No. Frances was the mother; she died in child-bed."

"Oh. But I thought — do you mean that her daughter was illegitimate?"

"Have you never heard of such a thing before?" asked Joel, amused by her flush of annoyance at being made to sound a simpleton. How those pock-marks stood out when the blood came up under the skin. It was a pity she was so badly blemished, for there were other things about her that were distinctly enticing. He wondered if her body was scarred as well, and whether he would ever get a chance to find out.

Philadelphia had no idea what was going on in his mind, she was too busy being surprised that the Tabors had been vulnerable to this particular misfortune. The climate of affection between them had always seemed to her cold, colourless and sterile, while their wealth appeared to protect them from any dangerous intrusion of the world outside. Had their daughter escaped deliberately or come to grief by accident?

"I wonder what happened," she said. "Do you know who was the father?"

"Some sprig of the nobility who came here to borrow money and ended by borrowing Frances as well. Unluckily he was married. She didn't care; she ran off with him and was never seen again. This is hearsay," added Joel, "for it was all over before we came here, and anyway I wouldn't have been more than seven years old at the time."

He was now twenty-three.

Edmund Beck came in from the shop. A well-meaning young man, pink-cheeked and ingenuous, he had become a goldsmith to please this mother. His elder brothers were with their father in the Mercers' Company, and the strong-minded Hannah had been determined that one of her children should carry on the traditions of her own family, so Edmund had been the unprotesting sacrifice, though he was not very deft with his hands and would rather have stayed on at school and gone to the university.

"Well, you've been working mighty hard," Joel greeted him. "I'd like to know whose plate it is you've been polishing. Have you any inkling how things are left?"

"My dear fellow, I wasn't the old man's attorney."

"I thought you might have been given a hint. It's of great moment to my father and me to know what he's done about the leasehold of this house, and the stock. Considering all things, he had a moral obligation to leave us a share — and it's not as though he had a natural heir to dispute our claim."

"No living descendant, it's true, but indirectly . . . "

"Ah, that's where you Becks come in! perhaps he's willed his entire property to you, Edmund. His wife's nephew."

Edmund looked slightly alarmed, and said quickly, "It's more likely he's willed it to Laurence."

"Laurence! Good heavens, I'll believe that when oranges grown on beanstalks."

Philadelphia was following this with interest. Laurence Tabor was the only son of the dead man's only brother. He

13.

had served his seven years' apprenticeship and then worked for his uncle until he ruined his prospects by quarrelling with the old man; he had either walked out or been thrown out, she was not sure which or why. This had happened six years ago, and she had been with the Tabors a mere eight months.

"Isn't it possible that he forgave Laurence?" she asked. "The sole inheritor of his name and blood? Why did they quarrel?"

"Laurence wanted to be a limner," said Edmund. "To paint those little miniature portraits that are worn in lockets and brooches."

"What was wrong in that? I thought limning was one of the branches of your craft. Mr. Hilliard is a goldsmith."

"You should have tried telling my uncle that — if you wanted your ears boxed. As far as he was concerned, a goldsmith was a smith working in precious metals and nothing more."

"Isn't that enough?" said Joel. "We're smiths first and foremost, that's the pride of our calling, and any other fanciful arts we learn are thrown in as a makeweight.

They weren't intended to save idlers like Laurence from doing their proper stint at the forge. He only pretended he wanted to paint because he didn't like getting hot and dirty. He's a smooth Italianate fellow, with hands as white as a woman's, always hoping to be taken for a gentleman; he even affected a lisp . . . "

"No, that's too bad," said Edmund, laughing. "You have got your knife into poor Laurence. When did you ever hear him lisp?"

"Well, then it was a drawl. What the devil does it matter? I don't care a fig for Laurence, so long as he stays over in Germany."

Receiving no comment from either of his companions, he began to make a speech.

"My father should have been recognised as John Tabor's partner years ago, only the cunning old brute always put off signing the agreement. It was a disgraceful way for one master-craftsman to treat another; my father was as good a goldsmith as Tabor, only he wasn't so lucky. He had his own shop once

— not in the Row, I grant you, but he had a place in Foster Lane where he was doing well enough until the house burnt down and we lost everything we had. It seemed very charitable of John Tabor to come to his rescue and settle all his debts. My father was so grateful, he agreed to everything that was suggested. He'd come here and work for low wages until he'd repaid the loan; I was to be bound apprentice to the old man, and Sam after me, and we were all to make our home under this roof — so that my mother lived and died in another woman's house, and my father lost his freedom and drudged on as though he was no more than a journeyman — but we were to swallow all this and look pleasant, because the old man had promised he should be a partner, and sooner or later he'd make it legal. Well, he never did, and now he's dead, and I want to know whether he put matters right in his will."

Edmund and Philadelphia had both heard this string of grievances before, especially during the last week, after Mr. Tabor's sudden illness took a turn for the worse, and there was no hope of his being fit to deal with any outstanding business matters.

It remained to be seen whether he had already made some sort of provision for Zachary Downes. He might have been prepared to sign an undertaking that would not be honoured until after his death. Alive, thought Philadelphia, he had not been noted for keeping his word. She considered her own experience of his large, vague promises.

The Whitethorns had lived on their own land in Gloucestershire for the last two hundred years. Quiet people, satisfied with their place in the world, they had not cared much for display until Philadelphia's brother William, marrying a little above him, had been persuaded that it was time their shabby old manor house was converted into something more like a gentleman's country mansion. Visiting London to raise money for this worthy object, he had met John Tabor, and during their negotiations he had apparently disclosed that one of his encumbrances was an unmarried sister of twenty-one who did not get on with his wife. Mr. Tabor had immediately offered

17

to take her into his own household, where she could make herself useful while he found her a suitable bridegroom.

It was quite a usual arrangement and Philadelphia had been glad to agree. She had no false pride about her birth and consequence; she knew that she would probably have a better life with a London merchant than with any of the squires who came within their orbit in Gloucestershire, and she was also anxious to get away from her sister-in-law. So she had come to Goldsmiths' Row, where she had been made very welcome and treated with great kindness — she had no complaints on that score — only John Tabor had never made the slightest mention of finding her a husband. After several weeks of feeling like a heifer at a fair whenever she went into company, it slowly dawned on her that none of the Tabors' friends had been given any customary hints about her dowry and connections. She suspected that Tabor had simply taken her in because he needed another woman in the house to be a companion to his ailing and rather foolish wife.

Not that he would have prevented my marriage, thought Philadelphia honestly if I'd found myself an eligible suitor. Any other girl would have known how to employ the opportunities I've had the last eight months, meeting the bachelor sons of all the wealthiest families in the City. Other girls didn't wait to have matches made for them, they went ahead and found their own lovers, giving rise to a great deal of headshaking by ancient persons who didn't know what the young women of today were coming to. But such girls were sure of their own success, flawless and desirable; they weren't branded like criminals with the horrible insignia of smallpox. Philadelphia had decided at fourteen that her face was going to be her misfortune. She had enough sense to know that there were men who would be willing to take a pock-marked wife, provided she fulfilled all the other conditions that a prudent bridegroom looked for. But the opening moves in a match of this sort were invariably made by the friends of the couple who wanted to bring them together. With no one to push her forward or take her part, she doubted whether she would ever get a husband.

She was not afraid of men; she was well able to treat them in a sisterly fashion, talking sensibly or making them laugh. And that was not likely to get her very far.

John Tabor's funeral took place three days later, and his will was read the following morning. The widow received a very handsome jointure: this was a foregone conclusion, for the amount had been stated in the terms of her marriage-settlement. There were a few small bequests, and everything else was left to 'my nephew Laurence on condition that he comes home to England and applies himself to his craft as a member of the Goldsmiths' Company.'

Zachary Downes received a legacy of twenty pounds and a mourning-ring.

He accepted this with resignation, as though he had expected nothing more. Joel was furious.

"That old villain, that lying hypocrite — I hope he's roasting in hell! I might have guessed he'd cheat my father, but I never thought we'd have Laurence lording it over us — why, the old man never had a good word to say for him. He only made that will last year; he must have been in his dotage."

"It's the old story, I suppose," said Philadelphia. "He decided that blood was thicker than water."

"The Tabors' blood must be thick with gold-dust."

"Suppose Laurence doesn't come home? The lawyers may not be able to find him."

"They know where he is already. He's taken good care to keep in touch," said Joel viciously. "Of course he'll come home. He won't find it very onerous keeping this shop so long as he has us to do all the work. And we've no choice; we can't afford to throw up our employment, and we haven't enough money to set up on our own account."

Philadelphia was very sorry for him, and hesitated before giving him a message from Mrs. Tabor, who was asking to see him.

"What's she want with me?" he demanded, on the verge of truculence.

"It's concerning her grand-daughter; I

think she wants you to go and fetch her."

"I'm damned if I will!"

"I understand how you feel, but do come and speak to her, Joel. It's certainly not her fault that your family was treated so badly."

He grumbled a little more, but finally went upstairs with her, and listened with impeccable civility when Mrs. Tabor told him how eagerly she looked forward to seeing her only grandchild.

"I would be very glad if you would act for me in this matter, Joel."

"I don't know that I can help you, madam. Where is your grand-daughter?"

"I am not precisely certain where she is now. Cicely Fox took her to live in Kent, and I suppose they are still there. I know you will find her and bring her to me as soon as you can. My little Frances! Only think, I have not had one single report of her since the letter Elizabeth wrote me the day she was born."

Joel and Philadelphia exchanged glances of baffled astonishment. They had assumed, from the confident way she spoke, that Mrs. Tabor must know exactly where the child was; probably with foster-parents chosen and paid by her grandfather.

"If you don't know were she is," said Joel slowly, "where am I to start looking? You can't expect me to search through the whole of Kent?"

"Why, no — poor Joel! Don't look so disconsolate. The whole of Kent, indeed! I have the name of the village, it is written down in the letter, as you shall see. Philadelphia, would you open the big chest under the window, and take out a coffer that is stowed away somewhere towards the bottom on the left, a little coffer made of Spanish leather . . . I keep the letter in there that Bess wrote me the day my dear daughter died. That was Elizabeth Angell, whose father had his shop at the other end of the Row, though they have all gone from there now, scattered heaven knows where. Bess must be more than thirty years old, for she and my Frances were exactly of an age, and it was to Bess that poor Frank turned, after that wicked man deserted her . . . "

Hunting in the big chest for the little

coffer, Philadelphia heard the whole story, which she translated in her own mind to a rational account of what had really happened.

Frances had run off to live blissfully in sin somewhere in the country, taking with her from Goldsmiths' Row her former nurse, a woman called Cicely Fox. The only other person in her confidence was her friend Bess Angell. When she was seven months pregnant her lover, Robin Martel, had surrendered to family pressure and gone back to his wife. It was not clear whether he had left Frances penniless or whether she had been too proud to accept his help. She had not approached her parents. It was Bess Angell who had secretly taken care of her, installing her and Cicely in a farm at Enfield belonging to her own family, but which they seldom visited. Mr. Angell only discovered what his daughter had been doing when he got an enquiry from the local coroner about a young woman who had died in his house. Horrified that Bess should be involved in such a scandal, he had carried her forcibly to relations in the West Country, and there she had remained. All Mrs. Tabor had received from her was this one letter.

Philadelphia had found it now; she offered it to her mistress, who asked her to read it aloud. She said her eyes were dim from weeping; Philadelphia had a suspicion that she had never entirely mastered the art of reading and writing.

The same might be said of Bess Angell, she reflected, unfolding the limp sheet of paper and trying to decipher the faded scrawl. There was no law which governed the way you chose to spell, that would be absurd, but most people did stick to a rough kind of orthodoxy. Not Bess Angell. She and her friend Frank, spoilt little heiresses, had no reason to waste their time on book-learning.

Madamm i greave to tel you deere Franke dyed in my armis . . .

Philadelphia was reminded that the writer of this letter was an eighteen-year-old girl who had just watched another girl through hours of agony that culminated in death. She was ashamed of her own arrogance. The letter was short and bleak. Frank had been in labour for thirty hours. The baby was strong and lusty. Frank had shown great courage. Then came the crucial part.

Shee axed me to care for her childe so I crissent the babby Fraunceys witch is al i cd do for feere of mi fathers rawth. Sisley and the babby ar lodjing with the wett nourse and wen Franseis is weand they wil goe to Sisleys kindread at Cobchirche.

Poor Mrs. Tabor was dabbing her eyes, but she must have brooded over these details so often that the pain was a little dulled. At the end she said, quite cheerfully, "There, you see. Cobchurch."

"Suppose she has the name wrong," said Joel gloomily. He had got a glimpse of Bess's handwriting.

"You need not trouble your head on that score, for I remember thinking, when I first had the letter, that Cobchurch in Kent was where old Reuben Fox came from forty years and more ago. He was a porter at the Shambles, and married a woman that worked for my mother as a laundress. Cicely was their daughter, who came to me when Frank was in her cradle. I know she had a brother who went back to their father's native village. So there's no doubt about Bess having the name right, and you should be able to find Cicely straight away, for it's only a small place where everyone is bound to be known."

There was a slight pause.

"Mrs. Tabor," said Philadelphia gently, "has it ever crossed your mind that the baby might have died?"

Mrs. Tabor was confident that little Frances had survived. She felt it in her bones. Philadelphia made another tentative suggestion.

"Should you not consider carefully before you bring her here? If she has lived all her life in a ploughman's cottage, she may not take kindly to Goldsmiths' Row."

"Then we'll go down to Hertfordshire and stay there until she is more used to our ways. It's true the great house at Thurley belongs to Laurence now, but

I don't suppose he'll object."

"Laurence!" said Joel sardonically. "Why not send him to hunt for your grand-daughter, madam? I'm sure he'll be more use to you than I am."

Mrs. Tabor became flustered. "Don't desert me, Joel — don't be angry. It wasn't my fault that there was no special provision — indeed it wasn't. I did try to suggest it, but he would not listen, and I am not very well instructed in such matters . . . But I'll tell you one thing I have always had in mind: that when my husband — if it pleased God that I should outlive him — I would offer a great reward to the person who found my Frances for me. And that is why I'm giving you the first chance to look for her, so that you can win the reward. It won't be as much as your father would have got from the partnership, but it will be worth having, I promise you."

Joel stared at her for a moment without speaking, and the anger died out of his face.

"Very well," he said eventually. "I'll go as far as Cobchurch for you, at any

28

rate. I reckon he was a hard master to you also."

"Oh, you must not say so," whispered Mrs. Tabor. But she did not contradict him.

3

JOEL sat astride a hired horse in the sodden desolation of a Kentish lane, gazing at a tumbledown cottage entirely surrounded by briars. The roof of mildewed thatch was full of holes, the place must have stood empty for years. He was calling down curses on the females of the Tabor family, and on all the yokels in the county of Kent without exception.

He had set off on his travels the previous day, well supplied with money and making the best of a tedious journey by dwelling on the promised reward. Having crossed London Bridge, he had asked a man in a carrier's cart the way to Cobchurch. Here things had begun to go wrong, for the carrier had sent him off in the direction of Orpington, to a place that turned out to be Cobstreet. Cobchurch, apparently, was somewhere quite different, over towards Rochester. He had turned eastwards, hammering along the bad roads as the day became darker and colder and he grew sore and stiff in the saddle, for he was not much of a horseman, and the old nag knew it and was giving him the devil of a jolting. The January dusk came down early. He put up at a wayside tavern where he was bitten all night by fleas. This morning, after several wrong turnings, he had at last reached Cobchurch, hungry for his dinner, only to discover that it was nothing more than a poor, scattered hamlet without so much as an alehouse.

A freezing wind was blowing from the direction of the North Sea and there was not a soul in sight. Joel supposed the inhabitants were all huddling inside their hovels to keep warm, for there was no one working in the common field — perhaps January was not the season for husbandry or any of their nasty occupations? Joel was a true Londoner, he hated the country and despised countrymen.

The first house he approached, they set the dog on him, and he had to fly for his life. He was hurrying away when he met a man plodding along with a sack wrapped round his head and shoulders like a kind of hood, whom he had now identified as the village idiot. (No one except the village idiot would have been out in such weather.)

Foolishly, Joel had asked this individual whether he knew Cicely Fox. The idiot had answered him with beaming smiles and sent him along a very dirty lane to the house which stood right at the end of it.

And here he was, faced with the dumb indifference of a desert ruin.

Unless it was the wrong cottage after all? That fellow under the sack must be clean out of his wits. Reviving a little, Joel turned and rode back along the lane. Presently he came to a small homestead with a duckpond and a few apple trees, and here there was a blessed sign of life: a woman fetching a bucket of water from the well.

Joel hailed her. "Can you tell me, mistress — the empty cottage down the lane, was there once a family called Fox living there?"

"Foxes ha' been done many a long day." She was a fat, comfortable body and at least she was not hostile.

"Are they still living in these parts?"

She shook her head and muttered something about Dan going for to make his fortune.

She had pushed open the door by now, and a thin crabbed voice came from inside the house. "Nan! Nan! Who are you gossiping with out there? bring the fellow in here, you silly wench."

"It's my father," explained Nan. "Best you come in. He's uncommon fratchety."

Joel was thankful for a chance to get out of the wind. He dismounted, hitched his horse's reins over the pump-handle, and stepped into the warm, cramped kitchen in which the smell of rabbit stew made him feel almost faint with hunger. The cooked rabbit and onions also helped to obliterate the other prevailing smells of tallow grease and old man.

The old man in question was crouched on a stool by the hearth, a desiccated gnome with a still fiery eye. He immediately wanted to know what Joel was after, accosting honest women and taking them from their work.

"He wants to find Dan Fox, Father."

"Not Dan," put in Joel. "A woman called Cicely Fox, whom I suppose to be his sister."

"And what's your purpose with that light-skirt? Not that it needs any guessing," added the gnome with a leer.

"Father, do mind your tongue."

Joel said with dignity, "It's a matter of business. She was once a maidservant in the household of a wealthy Cheapside merchant, and her evidence is needed in a matter of some concern."

The gnome gave a malignant cackle. "Reckon it was from that same merchant's house she came home with a lusty bastard for her wages. Came back as bold as brass, she did, the impudent strumpet."

"Now, Father — you know that happened a dozen years ago and more. And Cicely always denied the child was hers. She said the mother was her poor young mistress who died of grief because her sweetheart deserted her."

"More fool you, for believing such a tale."

Joel heard these exchanges with a certain relief. All through this uncomfortable odyssey he had been haunted by the thought that perhaps he ought to have gone first to Enfield, because it was quite possible that Frances Tabor's daughter had not survived her infancy. Now he knew that he was hunting the right line, at least Cicely had brought her as far as Cobchurch.

"What's become of these Foxes now?" he demanded.

Daniel had gone to work for his father-in-law, they told him, somewhere on the other side of the county. He had never been able to support his family on that sour land of his, let alone provide for Cicely and her brat. Not that Cicely had battened on him for long, she'd up and married Abel Perry that was tapster at the King's Head in Milstock.

"I came through Milstock this morning. Are the Perrys still there?"

"Not they. You wouldn't get that red-headed doxy to stay down here in the country. She nagged at Abel till he got work at a tavern in Southwark. Fox by name and vixen by nature, she was."

Joel's heart sank. Southwark was full of taverns. He asked, without much hope, whether they remembered where the Perrys had gone.

To his surprise, the old man did remember. He disliked the red-headed Cicely, it was ten years since she had left the district and nothing had been heard of her since, yet his mind was so starved of variety that he could still recall that Abel Perry had gone to an inn called the Rose of York. Joel paid him suitably for this information, and was given a helping of Nan's rabbit-stew, which revived him for his journey back to town. He devoured every morsel, cleaning the gravy off his trencher with hunks of dark bread, while the old cottager recited the sins and temptations of life in the suburbs of a great city. He seemed to know a surprising number of them.

By the time Joel reached Southwark, it was too late to continue his search; he wasted no time looking for the Rose of York, but installed himself at a more celebrated tavern, ordered a good supper, and then sallied out to commit a few of those sins so lovingly specified by the Cobchurch gnome.

Next morning he woke with a fore-boding of failure. It was true that he had escaped from the horrors of the countryside, but his chances of finding the Tabor grandchild were much diminished. In their native towns and villages even humble people like the Foxes and Perrys were known to everyone; once they came to a place like Southwark, they were just ants on a teeming anthill, and unless the tapster had stayed ten years at the same inn, it might be very difficult to trace him.

Southwark was a busy, sprawling borough, continually full of strangers and with three quite separate communities. The first and most notorious, established on Bankside and facing towards London across the Thames, were the providers of pleasure, safely stettled outside the jurisdiction of the Lord Mayor: the people from the theatres and the Paris Garden, the whores and gamesters, orange girls and bear-wards. Then there were those who catered for the constant stream of travellers between London and the Channel Ports: innkeepers, horse-keepers, wheelwrights, blacksmiths and all their fraternity. Finally, the largest group, the very poor artisans who did not belong to any of the Livery Companies and worked for a pittance outside the City bounds. A great many of them were foreigners; skinners, silk-weavers, glovers and particularly stone-masons.

Joel soon found that the Rose of York was a simple tavern in a back-street, whose patrons were chiefly shopkeepers and craftsmen.

There were no customers about so early in the morning, and he was able to question the landlord and his wife without interruption. Their name was Hodges and they were young people with their way to make; as soon as he saw them he knew they could not have been there long, and he was prepared for their answer; they had never heard of Abel Perry.

"Can you tell me who had the Rose of York before you?"

"An old couple of the name of Williams, been here for ever they had, until in the end the old fellow's aches and agues made his life such a burden that they gave up the Rose five years ago come Michaelmas, and went to live with a married daughter. Somewhere in the North Country, wasn't it, Meg?"

"Hundreds of miles away, that I do remember."

Joel groaned inwardly. Why did all these people keep moving about? Why couldn't they stay in one place?

"It's a fact," said the landlord, thoughtfully polishing a pewter jug, "that old Williams did employ a tapster after he began to fail, even though the takings here at the Rose don't warrant a servant's wages. But Perry? No, I never heard of a Perry, and I know most of the fellows in our trade. What did you want with him, sir?"

"It's a matter of inheritance."

They looked at him with respect, and Mrs. Hodges said suddenly, "It couldn't have been the poor souls that died, Jem? They that left the little orphan?"

"There was a child," said Joel, eagerly. "Go on, mistress, tell me more. Who were these people? What did they die of?"

"I had the story from some of the neighbours when we first came, sir. How old Jack Williams engaged a new tapster he met at a fair, a countryman who wanted to try his luck in Southwark. They didn't know much else about him or where he came from. He brought his wife and child with him and Williams gave them a lodging up in the attic. Well, it was a hot summer and the plague season in full spate, and these poor country folk not being so sturdy as we are, man and wife both took the disease and died the same night. And there was the child left with not a soul in the world to care for it."

"Do you know if it was a boy or a girl?"

Mrs. Hodges clearly did not know; she was repeating her dramatic story at third or fourth hand.

"It was a boy, I think. No, wait — it was little girl, and crying pitifully, poor mite, but too young to tell where she had come from, or whether she had any kinsfolk that would claim her. So what do you think Mrs. Williams did with her? Carried her round to the Charity Hospital and left her on the doorstep, and how any woman could be so wicked and heartless is more than I can tell."

"You are too hard on her, love," said Hodges. "She couldn't keep the child herself, she and her good man being old and sick, with enough troubles of their own. And as for leaving it on the doorstep, there's no doubt why she did that. If she'd gone to the Hospital openly and given them the whole history, the child might have been turned away because she wasn't born in Southwark."

"Never mind the rights and wrongs," said Joel. "You are telling me this tapster's infant was put into an asylum for orphan children."

"Yes, but whether the tapster was the man you want . . . "

"I'll have to look at the registers. Ten years ago — either seventy-eight or seventy-nine. What parish are you in?"

"St. Olave's," said Hodges. "That's a good notion of yours, sir. If it was the Perry's, you'll find their name among the burials."

And sure enough, as he pored over the parish register an hour later in the vestry of St. Olave's Church, and read through the long and melancholy list of deaths for the summer of 1579, he came across the entry he was looking for. '27th July. Abel Perry. Cicely Perry. Strangers.'

Joel felt a prickle of triumphant anticipation because he seemed to be nearing the end of his search.

Hodges had told him how to get to Webster's Charity Hospital, a foundation which had been endowed some thirty years ago by a pious old bachelor so that homeless children could be 'brought up in strict obedience, humble diligence, and the fear of the lord', according to a carved inscription over the door. The hospital consisted of three or four low brick houses built round their own courtyard. Joel was just about to knock on the main door when it opened, and a man came out. He was a severe, thin-lipped personage, plainly dressed in black and decidedly intimidating, though he addressed Joel pleasantly enough.

"What can I do for you, friend? I'm the Master of the Hospital."

Joel explained his errand.

"Frances Perry? I don't recall the name. But she must be past fifteen years by now, and no doubt she's been sent out to work as a serving maid or in some other lawful occupation. So I may never have seen her myself, for I've been here only a twelve-month."

(Like all the rest of them, thought Joel irritably. Jaunting about, never staying in one place.)

"However," continued the Master, "Mrs. Bullace will be able to help you. She's served the Lord in this place for more than twenty years, and has complete care of the girls. If this child has ever been through our hands, Mrs. Bullace will know where she is now."

These were cheering words. The Master then handed Joel over to a small orphan called Giles, who was commanded to take him straight to the Dame.

As he was led through various rooms of the Hospital, Joel stared around him with some curiosity. Though the whole place was solid and excessively clean, it was entirely without comfort. The stone floor were bare of rushes, and there were no fires. The girls who were sewing seams in one of the rooms were swaddled in scarves to keep warm; their hands were chapped and red. Joel's arrival was greeted with a chorus of high-pitched whispers, like the faint squeaking of mice. Then they all relapsed into a guilty silence. There were a few children skipping in the yard; even they were inordinately quiet. He supposed they must be in the male part of the Hospital, but just before the Dame's room they passed through one where there were some very small children, boys as well as girls, some in cradles, and one or two crawling about the floor. Sitting among them and rocking a tiny boy on her lap, was one of the most beautiful creatures Joel had ever seen.

She was about fifteen, her body rounded under a hideous, drab smock; her hair was scraped back and hidden by a cap, but a few fronds had strayed over her forehead, and they were the colour of white gold. She had an exquisitely heart-shaped face, and the drenching blue of her eyes was so brilliant that he was spellbound by her glance.

Then she flushed furiously, and turned away.

Joel was not a man who felt much

drawn by virginal innocence, but he was strangely affected by this vision. He had heard a good deal about the fairy-tale beauty of the runaway Frances Tabor; surely this must be her daughter, the girl he had come to find.

He was taken in to meet Mrs. Bullace. The Dame was a heavy, red-faced, elderly woman who looked more good-natured than the man Joel had encountered at the door. There was a hobby-horse and a Bartholomew lamb in one corner of the room, perhaps to be lent out as a special treat, and in front of a frugal fire a little girl with a cold was stroking a tabby kitten.

"You must go now, Deborah," said Mrs. Bullace, "for you see I have a visitor. Tell Grace that I said you might keep warm in the kitchen. And you may take Thomas Kitten with you."

Then she offered Joel a stool, and he settled down to tell her why he had come.

When he had finished, she shook her head sadly. "I fear I can do nothing for you, sir. We have never had your Frances Perry at the Charity Hospital."

"She might have been called by another name. Have you no Frances Tabor? or Frances Fox?"

"Neither. And I was not going by the name. It is simply that we never had a girl in our care who answers your description."

He was amazed. "How can you be so certain? So many children as you must have seen in the course of your time here, how can you remember them all without consulting your records?"

The woman smiled. She had an easy manner and a little more polish than he would have expected in such a place.

"We have twenty boys and twenty girls, and there is much coming and going. All the little ones are put in my care, for I have charge of the boys until they are turned four years, when they go to the Master's house, and the girls I keep as long as they remain with us. I wouldn't claim to recite a list of all the babies we have taken in, not if I had to give the exact dates and circumstances. But you are looking for a girl of five years old, and that's a different matter. Most of our infants are bastards, as you might expect, and some are left on the doorstep by night because their mothers are afraid to own them. But the children who come to us when they are older don't come as foundlings. They are the victims of misfortune whose parents have died or met with some disaster; we know all about them and exactly who they are."

"I understand," said Joel slowly. He felt curiously flat. "I can't make out what happened, though. If the innkeeper's wife brought the child here . . . "

Mrs. Bullace had no suggestion to offer.

After a moment, he said, "There was a girl I saw as I came in. She was minding the young babies. I suppose it's not possible . . . ?"

"That Grace Wilton should be your missing heiress? No, Mr. Downes, it is not possible. She came to us when she was a few weeks old, and there was no secrecy about her birth, for her mother was a Bankside harlot, and much frequented, I believe, until she died from eating oysters out of season."

"Oh," said Joel, disconcerted.

"Mind you," said Mrs. Bullace, "I pity Grace with all my heart. (You'll take a draught of cordial with me, sir? To keep out the cold?) I wish some family had adopted her when she was younger. It's too late now, and we can't send her out as a maidservant either."

"Why not?" he sipped the spicy, burning cordial she had poured for him, and wondered what was in it.

"Consider, Mr. Downes. What woman would take a bird of so bright plumage into her household if she had the virtue of her young sons to consider, let alone her husband?"

Joel saw the force of this. "So what will become of the poor girl?"

"She'll stay at the Hospital. We can use another pair of hands, and she's a good worker. But I'd like to see her safely settled before I go."

"Are you leaving the Hospital?"

It was no more than a civil enquiry; he was startled to find he had released a floodgate. You might well find a cause for astonishment, Mrs. Bullace informed him, that a woman should be turned off after twenty years' faithful service, just

48

because she was no longer so lightfooted as she used to be, and afflicted with shortness of breath — though everyone knew the real reason, how that sly fellow Silas Tucker, the new Master, wanted the Dame's place for his widowed sister; a couple of vinegar-voiced puritans they were, and the way they'd rule those unfortunate children it made your heart bleed to think of.

Here Mrs. Bullace took a gulp of cordial and defiantly put another log on the fire. Joel did not know what to say. She was certainly not drunk, though judging from the redness of her face, it was possible that the cordial was brought out fairly often. Its effect now was probably exaggerated by the pleasure of having a sympathetic listener. And perhaps the talk of a rich goldsmith's family, and the glories awaiting the lost Frances, had stirred an unaccustomed mood of discontent in the woman whose future must be so precarious. After as moment's pause she recollected herself. She brought the interview to an end by saying that it was nearly dinner-time and she had a great many hungry mouths to feed. She was sorry to have given him so little help.

Joel left the Charity Hospital without any clear idea of what to do next. He dined at an ordinary, and then went for a walk by the river.

It was a dry, frosty afternoon; across the sparkling water lay the familiar splendour of London, the great profile of St. Paul's and the endless streets of houses with innumerable church spires and towers rising out of them. St. Michael's and St. Peter's. St. Helen's and St. Andrew's, and the soaring pinnacle of St. Dunstan-in-the-East — he could have identified them all; he had known the churches of London by rote ever since he was a small boy playing Oranges and Lemons. Today he hardly saw they were there. He was trying to work out what could have happened to little Frances Tabor after the death of her foster-parents in 1579.

He finally decided that there were two probabilities. The account he had heard from the innkeeper's wife was vouched for, up to a point; the Perrys had certainly died very soon after their arrival at Southwark, but perhaps the picture of Mrs. Williams abandoning the child on the doorstep of the Charity Hospital was a myth? Suppose she had found a private family willing to care for the little girl; that would not have made nearly such a good story for the old gossips to moralise over in their cups.

There was a grim alternative. It was only too likely that Frances might have caught the plague from her foster-parents. She might have died on that doorstep, poor little wretch. He believed Mrs. Bullace when she boasted that she remembered all the girls she had brought up; he did not think she would remember the death of an anonymous waif at the height of the plague season. There were so many who died.

Either way, his search for Frances Tabor seemed to have ended in a blank wall, and he was convinced in his own mind that it was no good hoping to get any further.

Mrs. Tabor would be sorry. He was sorry too, for she was a good old soul, and he would have liked to find the grandchild who might have brought some comfort and colour to a life which must have been very dismal for a long time now. He would also have liked to earn the reward. In fact it was only now, with his hopes finally crushed, that he realised how much he needed that money. There were certain dreams he had been indulging, of himself and his father and Sam in a place of their own. Mrs. Tabor's reward — and perhaps Mrs. Tabor's continuing gratitude — would have provided a solid base to build on. Instead of which they would have to stay on indefinitely at Goldsmiths' Row, working for Laurence, and making do with the crumbs that fell from the rich man's table. Why was life so depressingly unlike the fairy-tales? Why couldn't little Frances have lived to become the ravishing beauty her grandmother had described so lovingly out of pure imagination, with her celestial blue eyes and golden hair?

A fantastic thought came into his mind, it was so audacious that it made him laugh. Such a plan could never succeed in a thousand years. A pity, for apart from all the other advantages, there would be a subtle revenge on John Tabor in the success of such a trick. And was it so hopeless, after all? He began to think it out, spent some time weighing up the pros and cons, and then went back to the Charity Hospital.

4

"YOU must be mad," said Mrs. Bullace. "I could never connive at such a scheme, it would be far too dangerous. However splendid the reward."

Joel was pleased to find that she did not produce any moral scruples. She simply objected to his plan because she thought the risks were too great.

"It's nowhere near so rash as you suppose," he assured her. "If I took Grace Wilton to Cheapside and presented her as my mistress's long-lost grandchild, I could offer plenty of proof. I could relate all the facts I have uncovered about the maidservant Cicely Fox, her marriage, and her death in Southwark ten years ago, and the story that the child was brought here to the Charity Hospital — every word of that is true. Then I could say that I came to you for help, and you told me of this young girl who was left at your door in the very month

54

of Cicely Perry's death. This would be our one positive lie, and I don't see who there is to dispute it, since you tell me that you are the only person now remaining who was at the Hospital so long ago — apart from some of the children who were no more than babies at the time. I don't think your word would be doubted, because I should then go on to suggest that Mrs. Tabor might question Grace — and this is the great strength of my plan: if Frances Tabor had indeed arrived here at five years old, she would have remembered some fragments of her life before she came; and I can provide Grace with as many memories as she needs to draw on. I can tell her a good deal about her foster-mother, and about the place in Kent where she lived for three years while Cicely's husband was working as a tapster at the inn. That's the only home the true Frances would have been able to recall, and neither Mrs. Tabor nor any of her family has ever been there. Even if Grace was caught out in some error, she could say that she didn't remember clearly, having been so young at the time. No imposter can ever have had an easier task, and you must understand that Mrs. Tabor longs to be convinced."

"You make it sound very simple," said Mrs. Bullace.

"It would be simple. Provided, of course, that the girl has wit enough to learn her part. Would she be capable of a little play-acting?"

"She's a hardened liar," said the Dame cheerfully. She met Joel's look of surprise, and laughed. "How else do you think our children could survive? Grace is a virtuous maid, but she will sometimes steal a spoonful of honey, or loiter a few minutes in the sunshine when she ought to be at her work. And then she'll lie to escape punishment . . . Still I doubt I ought not to encourage her in this present wickedness. Better for her to stay at the Hospital for ever than to enter on a life of deceit."

She did not sound very certain about it.

"Do you think she will stay here for ever?" asked Joel. "She's bound to stretch her wings in the end, and you can't keep her under lock and key; she must know already a little of what the world is like outside. You say you can't find her any lawful employment — well, there's plenty of unlawful employment for girls like her in Southwark of all places."

He felt that besides wanting the reward, Mrs. Bullace had a lively concern for Grace, and would rather have her committing perjury in Goldsmiths'Row than sinking under the corruption of a Bankside brothel.

After a few moments' thought, the woman said, "There's one question you haven't dealt with. If Frances Tabor had been brought here at five years old, she must have known her own name — or whatever name she was going under at that time; Frances Perry, most likely. She wouldn't have been called Grace Wilton. How were you going to explain that?"

Joel stared at her in dismay. This was a snag that had not crossed his mind. His wonderful design looked like foundering, because it would be impossible to conceal the name Grace had used all her life. Even the most casual enquiry at the Hospital would expose the truth; any one of the children would give it away.

The would-be conspirators cogitated

in silence. Oddly enough it was Mrs. Bullace who solved the difficulty.

"It can happen that when children of that age are left suddenly among strangers, their confusion and distress is so great that they lose the power of speech. If your Frances had been abandoned after the death of her foster-parents — yes, I think she might have been struck dumb long enough for us to have chosen a new name for her and taught her to accept it."

Joel was a little dubious, but he decided that Mrs. Bullace was probably right; she must know a lot about children, after all.

Mrs. Bullace was so pleased with her own cleverness that she gave up her objections. Somehow, imperceptibly, it became certain that she was ready to take part in the plot.

There was one other person whose complicity was even more important. Joel waited on tenterhooks while Grace Wilton was fetched. She represented his last hope of getting Mrs. Tabor's reward; a fraction at least of the money that his family were entitled to and needed so badly.

When she came into the room, he was astounded, all over again, by the sight of her. She really was a most ravishing creature, with her straight nose and soft little mouth, her rose-petal complexion and those celestial blue eyes. He did not imagine she was very much like her supposed mother, apart from the commonplace similarity of fair hair and blue yes, but he was sure she was just what old Mrs. Tabor had been dreaming of — not only beautiful but unworldly, for the Charity Hospital had certainly stamped on any pretensions to vanity, and he had never seen such a pretty girl who seemed so little aware of herself.

She gave him one glance of speculation when she first came in, and then stood respectfully in front of Mrs. Bullace, with her hands clasped and her eyes lowered, as she had been taught.

"Now, Grace: I have some good news for you," began the Dame. "How would you like to go and live in a great house on Cheapside?"

"I should like it very well!" She had a very young, flute-like voice which rose to a squeak of excitement. "If you please, mistress, am I to be a laundress or kitchenmaid?"

"Neither one not the other. You are a very fortunate girl, for you are going to perform a more valuable service. Not through any particular merit on your part, but because there is a wealthy widow who has lost her grand-daughter, and it so happens that you greatly resemble her."

"If it please you, mistress — what will I have to do?"

"You will have to pretend that you are the lost grand-daughter, call yourself by her name, and also — it may be — use some other small deceptions; there's nothing to fear, Mr. Downes here will tell you what to say."

"Is the poor lady out of her wits?"

It had struck Joel several times, especially during his sojourn in Kent, that Mrs. Tabor was undoubtedly out of her wits. However, she was not mad in the sense that Grace intended, and he hastened to explain that she was very melancholy because her husband had just died, that she longed for the company of the grandchild she had never seen, and surely it would be a kind action to make her happy again?

"And you would not be the loser," he added. "Think of it, Grace — you would live in a splendid house in Goldsmiths' Row, and have a great many fine dresses and eat your dinner off a silver plate. And you would go shopping at the Royal Exchange, and to all manner of feasts and revels . . . "

Grace was staring at him, round-eyed, quite forgetting the rules of Charity Hospital behaviour. "If it please you, sir — how long will they let me stay in that house?"

"Why, you'd stay there for ever. At least," he corrected himself, "until they found you a handsome young bridegroom. You'd like that, wouldn't you?"

The girl looked more perplexed than delighted. She turned to Mrs. Bullace, as though expecting some sort of guidance, but Mrs. Bullace was refreshing herself with a sip of cordial.

"Do you mean," said Grace at last, "that I am to go on all my life pretending to be that rich lady's grand-daughter? But that would be acting a lie! It would be wicked!"

Joel was disconcerted. Mrs. Bullace intervened in a magisterial tone, her colour rather heightened.

"That's enough of your presumption, my girl. Who set you up as a judge? Do you think that anything I allowed you to do would be wicked?"

"No, mistress. I ask your pardon, mistress. I'm very sorry."

Grace twisted her hands, immediately awkward and placating.

Mrs. Bullace spoke quietly to Joel.

"You had better leave her to me. I'll soon persuade her that I know what's wisest for her to do. In the meantime, if Silas Tucker asks me, I shall tell him we are convinced that Grace Wilton is the girl, and you have gone to consult with your patron; Tucker won't know any better, for he's only been here a twelve-month. If you come back tomorrow, I believe this foolish child will be happy to fall in with our plans."

5

GRACE WILTON was stooping over the tub in the laundry, her sleeves rolled above the elbow, as she dealt with a mountain of dirty clothes, rubbing and dipping and squeezing and wringing — it was heavy work but she was used to it, and at least you kept warm. The laundry itself was a chilly outhouse opening on to the yard, but the water was hot, she had staggered across with two buckets of it, straight from the kitchen fire; the tingle of comforting warmth ran upwards from her wrists, and she was wrapped in a cloud of steam.

She was still trying to get clear in her mind the extraordinary interview she had just had with Mrs. Bullace and the strange man from the City. She could hardly believe that it had really happened. It seemed incredible that she might actually find herself being taken to live at a rich merchant's house in Cheapside. Yet even more astonishing than this fairy-story promise of wealth and splendour was the fact that Mrs. Bullace was encouraging her to tell lies. She was so dumbfounded by this that it almost overshadowed the glories of Goldsmiths' Row.

Grace was not a very truthful girl; she was not at all brave, a grave disadvantage for any child growing up in the hard conditions of the Charity Hospital. Perpetually trying to cover up her misdemeanours, she would say almost anything to avoid a whipping. This also had its dangers, for being caught out in a lie was one of the worst crimes in the calendar. Yet here was Mrs. Bullace, after all her severe admonitions, suddenly turning round and saying that Grace ought to pretend she was this rich girl who had disappeared and tell all sorts of stories about people and places she had never heard of. It was very mysterious and she could not make it out; perhaps Coney would understand, and help her decide what to do.

Coney was the person Grace loved most in the world. He was supposed to be a year older than her — though ages at the Charity Hospital were never very exact — and they had been friends since they were about five or six years old. Although the boys and girls were brought up in separate houses, they were allowed to play together in the yard, and she remembered Coney as a champion at leapfrog, handstands and spinning the top. He could invent wonderful games too; he had brought imagination and liveliness to a drab setting, where many of the children were dull from lack of affection.

For some time now Coney had been going out to work. He was not apprenticed to any trade; orphans and foundlings could not count on such advantages. Coney had picked fruit and hoed turnips, held horses and run errands; since last summer he had been employed as a servant by a Dutch stonemason, Melchior Breda, one of the many foreign Protestants who had fled from persecution on the Continent and who thronged the London suburbs, a cheap labour force that was not very welcome inside the City boundaries. Melchior Breda carved tombstones and memorials; he lived alone in one small room in Southwark, so Coney still came home to sleep at the Charity Hospital, and when he arrived he would usually seek out Grace, especially if she was working somewhere out of the public eye.

Presently she heard the latch lift, and the door opened, letting in a draught of freezing cold air, for though it was only five o'clock, the January night had already begun. Coney stepped out of the darkness into the faintly quivering light of the lantern. He was a sturdy boy with a merry, stubborn face and thick, fair hair; he owed his strange nickname to the rabbit-skin hood he had been wearing when he first arrived at the Hospital. Stubborn even then, he would not be parted from it, though it was the height of summer. The name had stuck, but the origins were forgotten; he was nearly as tall as a man now and still growing; his arms shot out of the sleeves of his old jerkin, which was powdered with white dust, because he spent so much of his time heaving about great blocks of stone.

"Oh, Coney! I'm so glad you've come."

He looked at her anxiously: he was always trying to protect her from hardships which he could accept quite cheerfully himself.

"Is anything wrong?"

"No, at least I'm not in any trouble — not yet — I just don't know what to do, it's all so strange, and I can't for my life make out why Mrs. Bullace should want me to do such a thing."

"Of all the hen-witted girls! Can't you say what you mean?"

Grace laughed. She regarded this as a term of affection. "Listen and I'll tell you . . . "

Coney listened, absently helping her to hang out the washing on a line which ran across the width of the laundry. By the time she had finished he had forgotten about the clean shirts, his attention was riveted.

"Of all the cunning schemes! That Downes must be a fox and no mistake."

"Yes, but why does Mrs. Bullace want me to do what he says? That's the part I can't fathom."

Coney thought for a moment. "I expect he's promised her a share in the reward."

"What reward?"

"Why, for finding the lost heiress. If this rich old woman is so anxious to discover her grand-daughter, she's bound to have offered one. Yes, and if Downes can't find the real girl, he won't get anything, so I dare say that's why he hit on this notion of putting you in her place."

Grace listened respectfully. Coney spent his working hours in the great world outside the Charity Hospital and this gave him the status of an oracle. But there was one point she was inclined to cavil at.

"Even if there is a reward, surely Mrs. Bullace wouldn't . . ."

"She might, if it's true that Tucker means to get her turned out so that his sister can come here as Dame. She must want money, or what's to become of her?"

"I don't know," said Grace. Poor old Mother Bullace, she was often rough and sharp, but she could be warm-hearted too, and a provider of small pleasures, she would be very much missed. All the same, there was another and more urgent question to be solved.

"What do you think I ought to do?" she asked Coney.

"You'll refuse, won't you? It would be crazy to fall in with such a plot." He sounded surprised. "Surely you can see that? You can't live under a false name, and take things that don't belong to you . . . "

"I don't see why not. If that old woman gave them to me."

"She'd only do it if she thought you were her own kith and kin. And what about the real grandchild? You'd be stealing her birthright."

"Mr. Downes says she's been dead for ten years. So I don't see why it would be wrong, if I made her grandmother happy — why shouldn't I be happy too? Why shouldn't I get away from this prison, it's the only chance I'll ever get," wailed Grace on a note of despair.

"Poor Grace, don't cry," said Coney full of awkward concern. "It's wretched for you having to stop here, but it won't be for ever, I promise. You know I'm going to marry you when we're older and I can earn a living for us both . . . "

"But that won't happen for years and years! And they won't even allow us to meet; remember what happened at Michaelmas. You'll soon forget me, once you live outside the Hospital."

"I'll not forget," said the boy stolidly. It crossed his mind that if she went to live in Goldsmiths' Row, she would soon forget him. Was this why he felt so righteously indignant at the thought of Grace cheating the merchant's widow? Not entirely, he decided. There was the risk that she might be found out and sent to prison.

He was beginning to say this when she silenced him with a movement of her hand.

There was a footfall in the yard outside.

"Someone's coming — quick, you must hide!"

Frantic they gazed around. The back of the outhouse was full of shadows; there were several hampers stacked by the wall. Coney dived behind one of them, just as the door opened, and Grace was appalled to see the gaunt black figure of Silas Tucker, Master of the Charity Hospital.

"Grace Wilton! What are you doing out here so late?"

"If it please you, sir, there was such a lot of washing today."

"You'd work faster if you didn't waste your time in profane dreaming and idleness. Has there been anyone out here with you? I could swear I heard voices."

"If it please you, sir, there were some men in the lane just now. I think they were drunk," said Grace in a moment of inspiration, "for their language was very lewd."

She did not know how she had managed to bring out this red herring, for she was almost too terrified to speak. She was anticipating what would happen if Coney was found hiding behind the laundry hamper. It was a matter of conviction to Mr. Tucker that if a boy and girl were left alone together, their natural wickedness would inevitably cause them to sin. There had been a terrible retribution last Michaelmas, after she and Coney had slipped out quite innocently to go for a walk by the river. Mr. Tucker had himself administered the beatings which followed, and he had been entirely without pity. As she stood before him now in the damp wash-house, Grace was quaking with fright and certain that the signs of guilt must be written all over her face.

But apparently he accepted her story about the men in the lane, and perhaps he thought she was shivering from the cold, for he merely told her to get back indoors.

"There are plenty more tasks to be done, and if I hear of you loitering again, I will make you sorry."

"If it please you, sir, I will do my best, sir," stammered Grace, humble and servile.

In spite of her servility she was coming to a decision. Like Coley, she realised the risk she would run if she attempted to pass herself off as the missing Frances Tabor. These risks would have been quite enough to daunt her if she hadn't been reminded how confined and miserable and hopeless her position was at the

Charity Hospital. It was not so bad being here when you were a child, and most of the orphans escaped as they grew up, but she had never been given an opportunity until now. So she was going to seize it while there was still time, she was going to try her luck in Goldsmiths' Row.

6

"NO, I do not find it a cause for rejoicing," Mrs. Beck crossly informed her sister, "that you are proposing to take in some nameless pauper waif who has the impudence to pretend that she's your grandchild . . . "

"I am sure she must be my grandchild. Joel has traced her all the way from Cobchurch to Southwark, and found out that she was put in the Charity Hospital, poor mite, after Cicely died."

"So he says. Don't you understand, Alice, that he has given you no proof of his story? How you came to trust him with such an enterprise, a mere journeyman, an underling . . . "

"Zachary Downes and his boys are friends of long-standing; John trusted them . . . "

"Not enough to leave them a share in the shop. Arthur was appalled when he heard of your imprudence. Surely you could have consulted him first?"

"No, I couldn't," said Mrs. Tabor with unusual asperity, "because Arthur would never have attempted to find Frances, he would simply have come over here and told me how foolish it would be to start looking for her."

"So it was foolish," persisted Mrs. Beck. "Even supposing this girl is Frank's child — which I absolutely refuse to believe — even so, there's no place for her here. A mannerless, untaught bastard, dragged up in penury with a pack of children from the gutter — how do you think she will conduct herself in Goldsmiths' Row? You'd be wiser to leave well alone."

Mrs. Tabor burst into tears.

Hannah Beck was made rather uneasy by her sister's distress, but she was too thick-skinned to be a very successful comforter.

"There, Alice, it's no good crying over spilt milk. What's done can't be undone. I'll leave you now to consider what I've said, I'm sure you'll remember how often I've given you good counsel. Mrs. Whitethorn, I believe you had something to give me for Judith? A pattern for a stomacher, was it?"

With many cryptic winks and nods, Mrs. Beck signified that she wanted to speak to Philadelphia in private.

Directly they were outside the door of Mrs. Tabor's bedchamber, she said, "My sister seems to set great store by your opinion. You must discourage her from paying any attention to this imposter. We don't want her to be made the victim of a plot."

"Certainly not. But if you will forgive me, madam, I don't see how you can be certain that this girl is an imposter. Why shouldn't she be your niece's child, after all? Surely you don't mean to condemn her out of hand?"

"I can recognise a tissue of lies when I hear them. Mr. Beck and I are convinced that this so-called foundling is an adventuress, hoping to take advantage of my sister's credulity. And I think you will admit that we have more experience of the world than you. I don't know how these things are judged in the deserts of Gloucestershire, but here in London it is considered very impertinent for an unmarried woman to give advice to her elders and betters. My sister allows you great licence, but your position here is a humble one, in which you ought to be seen and not heard."

Philadelphia felt herself go hot and cold with mortification. It was intolerable to be patronised like an ignorant rustic by this complacent shopkeeper's wife, and as much as the attack on her good manners she resented the slur on her good sense. Of course she saw the danger of a wealthy woman like Mrs. Tabor offering to hand out large sums of money to anyone who could provide her with a grandchild she had never seen. She knew that Joel was very eager to win the reward; had he been too ready to accept the claims of any girl who was put forward as the missing heiress? From what Philadelphia could make out, he had been hunting for Frances Tabor through the taverns of Southwark, where every kind of gull-groper and trickster congregated, and the bait of Mrs. Tabor's wealth would have been enough to produce half a dozen false heiresses.

On the other hand, if Joel had gone to look for Frances in the right place, why shouldn't he have found her? It would be absurd to reject her in advance.

That evening Philadelphia and Zachary Downes were waiting upstairs in the great chamber with Mrs. Tabor when they heard the hired coach draw up in the street below. She had agreed to the presence of these two witnesses at her first meeting with her supposed grandchild, because she felt they were on her side, and would help to put a spoke in Hannah's wheel. She was breathing rather fast as she sat watching the door. They heard Joel's voice on the staircase, rallying someone to keep her courage high, no one was going to eat her.

The door opened, and there was Joel, surveying them with a faintly aggressive air; he must know that any suspicion of the claimant he had produced so conveniently was bound to reflect on him. But they hardly had time to consider Joel; they were all staring at the girl who stood trembling beside him. She was very young and fragile, swamped in a borrowed cloak, and her hair, brushed back from her forehead, was like spun gold. She had small, delicate features and a rose-petal complexion; her eyes were filled with fear and curiosity. They were the deepest sea blue.

"Why, she's the image of my Frank!" exclaimed Mrs. Tabor. "She's Frank over again!"

Philadelphia took this with a grain of salt. All the same, the words gave her a queer prickle of excitement.

"Come closer, child," Mrs. Tabor was saying. "And tell me how much you can recall of your early childhood. And first of all, what is your name?"

"If it please you, madam, my name is Frances. But they call me Grace."

"How strange! Why is that?"

"If you please, madam, they said that Grace was more fitting for an orphan brought up on charity."

Was there a flicker of an eyelid for Joel here; to see whether she had made the right reply? Philadelphia could not be sure. The girl was undoubtedly very nervous, perhaps she was merely over-awed by her surroundings. She had moved forward and bobbed a little curtsy, the sort that a poor man's child would be taught to make. Her

79

voice was low and pleasant. She spoke with much the same accent as the City people (who all sounded equally quick and clipped to Gloucestershire-born Philadelphia). Her manner was respectful and reserved; she might have grown up in Southwark, but the Charity Hospital had sheltered her from the loud, rough manners of the teeming streets and all their bawdy vulgarity.

She was answering Mrs. Tabor's questions about the woman who had first taken care of her.

"I called her Nurse. She was fat and laughing, and she had red hair."

"Cicely Fox had red hair," said Mrs. Tabor, beaming with pleasure.

The soft voice went on: "I don't think I ever knew my mother, madam. Nurse told me that she was a beautiful young lady who used to live in a house that was covered all over with gold."

Mrs. Tabor gave a gasp of delight. This was proof enough for her, she needed no more convincing. Philadelphia glanced sideways at Joel and caught him gazing at his Galatea.

"Did you ever see such a little beauty?"

he murmured as an aside to Philadelphia.

She was struck by the quiver of admiration in his voice. No man would ever look at her with just that rapt expression, or turn and stare after her in the street as they would stare at this little honey-sweet creature, who was probably a liar and possibly a strumpet. Philadelphia pulled herself up sharp. She had no right to think evil of the child, just because she was jealous. It was one thing to have an indelibly scarred face; fifty times worse to let the ugliness turn sour in the mind. That was something to avoid at all costs.

She had wanted the foundling's claims to be true, because of the happiness this would bring to Mrs. Tabor, and also because it would be a crushing defeat for Mrs. Beck. Now she had a third reason. Her natural generosity demanded that the girl she secretly envied must be given the benefit of every doubt.

7

GRACE lay stiffly at the edge of the bed she was sharing with Mrs. Philadelphia Whitethorn, and tried to keep perfectly still and to breathe without making a noise — she did hope she wouldn't snore. Not that she was unused to sharing a bed; in fact, she would have been frightened if they had put her in a room by herself, but Mrs. Whitethorn was rather alarming. She must be over twenty years old and still unmarried, getting on for an old maid, with those smallpox scars on her forehead, yet she was elegant and pretty, and she moved so beautifully and talked in such an easy, confident voice; Grace found it almost impossible to answer her, though she probably meant to be kind.

Mrs. Whitethorn seemed an altogether superior being. She spent far more time brushing her hair and saying her prayers than Grace had ever spent over either, and she had a special ball of soap for cleaning her teeth, and a special shift to wear in bed. Grace, who had gone to bed naked all her life, was amazed by this garment which was made of the most delicate white lawn, with goffered frills at the throat and wrists. She was amazed by the warm, scented rose-water that had been brought for them to wash in, and which had left a luxurious fragrance on her skin, she could smell it as she lay inside the great curtained bedstead, the size of a small room. The linen sheets had been aired by a warming-pan, and the feather bed was so soft, it was like lying on a cloud.

If the bedchamber afforded such marvels, the other rooms had been even more bewildering. She had always lived in a place where the barest necessities had been counted out — there were just enough stools for everyone to sit down, and just enough knives for everyone to cut their meat, and if you needed anything like a needle and thread to do the mending, Mrs. Bullace would get it out of a locked casket. If you lost or broke the needle, you were punished for it, because carelessness was a sin and needles cost money. But here in Goldsmiths' Row they must live by quite a different set of rules. There seemed to be an unlimited number of things for the use of everyone; there were more candles than Grace had ever seen alight at the same time; and as for the many rich dishes they had at supper, she hardly knew what she was eating.

She had not been given a silver plate but they all drank out of silver cups and on the centre of the table there was a silver-gilt salt, about a foot high and shaped like a lantern with pictures from the Bible embossed on the sides.

"That was your grandfather's masterpiece," Mrs. Tabor told her. "The piece he had to submit to the Goldsmiths' Company when he applied for recognition as a master of his craft."

Her grandfather! Of course John Tabor was not really her grandfather, and this brought home the wickedness of all the lies she had repeated. Though she did not find it difficult to enter into the part of the unknown Frances; the things that had happened to her did not seem at all alien, and she found herself almost believing in what she said. She had always been able to imagine things in a game, that was why she had got on so well with Coney.

Coney had been so angry and scornful about her coming to Goldsmiths' Row; he had called her a cheat and a thief and refused to say good-bye to her. She had pretended not to care at the time, but now, cast adrift in this complicated new world, she felt desperately alone, and began wondering if she would ever see him again. The thought was too much for her, and she began to cry.

She sobbed undisturbed for a few minutes, and then a voice from the other side of the bed asked her what was the matter. "Do you feel ill? Or just miserable?"

"Oh no, madam. I'm very h-happy," gulped Grace.

It had instantly flashed across her mind that tears might be taken as a symptom of guilt, a proof that she was an imposter.

But Philadelphia Whitethorn merely said, "You're homesick."

"Yes, I think I must be a little. Though it's very strange, for I was heartily glad to leave the Charity Hospital. Only there were some of my friends . . . "

"I know. You don't have to tell me. My first night in this room, when I came here last year, I cried my eyes out."

"Did you?" Grace was astounded, and also puzzled by Mrs. Whitethorn's exact status. "Do you live here all the time, madam?"

"Yes, I came from the country to act as a waiting-woman to your — to Mrs. Tabor. And by the same token, there is no need for you to treat me so formally. I have a confoundedly long name which you can use, but most people shorten it to Del."

It was an eye-opener to Grace that a gentlewoman could be a kind of servant; perhaps that was why she had cried?

"I longed to come to London, and live in Goldsmiths' Row," said Philadelphia, "for I knew I should like to be at the hub of things and meet so many different people, and I was not very happy sharing a house with my sister-in-law, who is always cross. But it was my home, after all, and I missed the familiar faces and places when I came away. Just as you are doing now. You'll feel better when you wake up in the morning."

She was right, as Grace gratefully discovered. By daylight she began to get her bearings in the large, impressive building. The ground floor at the front was taken up by the shop: there was a room that opened on to the street, and another where favoured customers could sit and examine the goods at their ease. Grace, peeping in, saw Joel Downes spreading a sable velvet cloth over the table and displaying against the inky blackness a shining set of Apostle spoons for the inspection of some people who had come to choose a christening present.

Behind the shop was the workshop, and that was just as fascinating. It was like a kind of kitchen, because of the furnace, which was a rectangular stove projecting from the wall under its own hooded chimney-piece. There was a pair of organ-bellows fitted into the side wall to bring up the fire, and a circular opening on the flat top of the stove, called the wind-hole. The furnace had to be very fierce; it was used for melting down old pieces of plate, and for annealing

— heating metal until it became pliable — so that it could be cut into shape and worked on the anvil.

Once a piece had been hammered into shape, and any necessary joins made with a soldering alloy, it was generally decorated with an embossed work or engraving. An old journeyman called Ralph stood all day at his bench between the furnace and the window, silently wielding his gravers and chasing hammer. The workshop was very hot and smelt of scorching metal and of various strange minerals, from the jars of pickle in which the finished pieces of plate were left soaking, to clean them before they were burnished with leather buffers and fine sand.

Grace was soon sharing the everyday work of the house. She was frightened of the servants, who were at first inclined to despise her, but when they found she was a painstaking diligent girl who didn't try to put on airs, they relented and were very kind to her. She found that she was expected to do only the pleasantest chores. She had to sew a little (and she was already an accomplished needlewoman), learn how to make pastry and other delicate feats of cookery, and help Philadelphia with the marketing.

She was given a beautiful dress and cloak, the first new clothes she had ever possessed. They had to be black, because of the mourning for John Tabor, but Grace did not mind, she was so entranced with the richness of the stuff, and the thick, quilted petticoat, which made her feel almost as though she was wearing a farthingale hoop, like a court lady. She had a black felt hat, and a pair of black leather shoes from the cordwainer, and to complete this dream of perfection, a short chain dangling from her waist with a purse and a polished looking-glass and a pair of scissors made of Toledo steel.

The only fly in the ointment was bustling, censorious Mrs. Beck, who was perfectly certain that Grace was not her great-niece.

"Do you know what happens to girl who tell lies?" she demanded at their second meeting.

"Yes, madam, they burn everlastingly in hellfire."

Grace then had to step back hastily, to avoid getting her ears boxed for impudence. She had not meant to be impudent. It was the proper answer for the question when it was asked at the Charity Hospital, so she knew it must be true, though she was much more frightened of what would happen to her in this world, if she was found out.

"Mrs. Tabor has had many sorrows," Philadelphia said to her one day. "It would be a great pity if she was made the victim of a cruel jest. I dare say she might be cozened out of a fair sum of money without feeling the pinch, but I think she would be greatly hurt by the unkindness."

Grace felt a shock of compunction mingled with fear, and very nearly gave herself away. Instinctively, she slid into the cloud of evasion which had been her best safeguard throughout her life at the Charity Hospital.

"I wish I could prove that I am Frances Tabor," she said gazing candidly at Del. "I wish I could swear it on my Bible oath. But I can't remember were I was born. I can remember my foster-parents dying in the attic room above a tavern, but I don't know their proper names, or the date, or how long afterwards that woman left me on the step outside the Charity Hospital. How could I understand what was happening when I was five years old?"

8

IT must be hard, thought Philadelphia, to have no identity, only a procession of confused memories with no one to interpret them. However much the evidence pointed her way, it was true that Grace could not actually swear, of her own knowledge, that she was Frances Tabor.

Philadelphia was inclined to believe that Grace was the full heiress, and although she was in no hurry to state her definite opinion, she found herself inadvertently doing so, rather sooner than she expected.

It was a February afternoon, about three weeks after Grace's arrival. The two girls had intended to go for a saunter round the haberdashers' booths in the Royal Exchange, but the sky was so dark and rainy that they paused in the doorway of the shop, wondering if they had time to get to Bishopsgate before the deluge. They had just finished dinner, there were very few people about, and the men were all in the workshop.

As they lingered on the threshold, Philadelphia heard a slight noise which made her glance round. There was a man in the adjoining room, the inner sanctum where favoured customers were taken to make their purchases in comparative privacy. This particular customer had got rather more privacy than he was entitled to. He was alone, standing with his back to them, and calmly helping himself to a cluster of gilded chains that hung from a hook on the wall. Philadelphia trod lightly across the space between them and stopped within six inches of his elbow.

"Can I be of any service to you, sir?"

The stranger jumped visibly and swung round to confront her. He was a slender young man, rigged out with all the glories of an absurdly tall beaver hat, a cloak lined with quilted satin and a pair of scented gloves. He had handsome, regular features and a small, pointed beard. His light grey eyes had a supercilious expression, and he wore a single pearly ear-ring.

93

If she had startled him, he soon recovered; he looked her up and down and enquired with extreme civility, "What kind of a service had you in mind, madam?"

Philadelphia was slightly baffled by his air of ease and fashion, and also by the fact that he probably thought she was another customer — she was dressed for the street. All the same, she had been warned about the effrontery of the accomplished London thief, and the way he had picked up the necklaces and slung them casually over his arm was carrying impudence a little too far.

"I thought you might wish to make a purchase," she said, "and since I am staying in the house . . . "

"You are?" There was a flickering change of expression; was it fear? Regrettably, it was more like amusement. "I hope you aren't gong to send for the constable?"

"Why, no. I never — that is to say . . . "

"You would find it very difficult," said the young man gently, "to prefer a charge."

Philadelphia came to her senses, feeling every kind of fool.

"You're Laurence Tabor!" she said accusingly.

"Yes. I should have told you so straight away. But I wasn't expecting . . . "

He broke off, having now caught sight of Grace. He stood gazing at her in rapt admiration. Moonstruck, like all the rest, thought Philadelphia irritably. She decided to give him a surprise in return.

"I must present your new kinswoman to you," she said. "She is the daughter of your cousin Frances, or so we believe, and I am sure you will be glad to make her acquaintance."

For a moment he was speechless. When he found his voice, all the light, teasing humour had gone out of it.

"Frank's child? Who says so? Has everyone here gone mad? I can see it's high time I came home to protect my aunt from such effrontery."

Grace turned as white as a sheet and began to tremble.

"Oh Del, what will happen to me? What will he do?"

"Nothing," said Philadelphia. "There's nothing he can do; your fate isn't in his hands."

A natural instinct to defend the weak had made her take Grace's part. She knew that she ought not to have spoken as though Grace's claims were already established, but in spite of this, she said fiercely to Laurence, "You have no cause to be so discourteous. Or so unjust."

He did not answer, but walked towards the door that led to the back premises, and shouted: "Shop!"

Joel came hurrying through, saw Laurence, and stopped dead. "So it's you."

"The rolling stone, as you see. How are you Joel?" He held out his hand.

Joel ignored this approach, perhaps deliberately or perhaps because he had now caught sight of Grace, who had begun to cry.

"What's been going on here?" he demanded, with a touch of alarm.

"You may well ask. I came home to Cheapside and walked straight into Bedlam."

"If you'd let us know when to expect you . . . "

"You wouldn't have left the shop unattended," said Laurence agreeably.

"We've hardly finished dinner," protested Joel, tugging at his starched white collar. "And Sam's about somewhere. We have been taking the greatest care of your property, never fear."

The two young men faced each other with a cat-and-dog hostility. Joel was the dog, of course, large and burly, with his blunt, engaging features. Laurence, in his foreign clothes, had something exotic and catlike about him.

After a moment he said, "I must go to my aunt."

"I'll take you to her," offered Joel.

Philadelphia noted that they were united in their desire to escape from Grace's tears.

They had hardly passed through the curtained archway that led to the staircase, when Laurence's voice floated back into the shop.

"Joel, who the devil are those girls?"

Grace began to wail. "Oh, what shall I do? What will become of me?"

97

"Hush," said Philadelphia. She was listening, all ears.

" . . . No, don't tell me she's my legendary cousin. Who is she in sober fact? How did she get here? Did that other wench bring her?"

"She got here because your aunt sent for her; no doubt you'll be told all the circumstances. And the other wench is Mrs. Tabor's attendant, a young gentlewoman of very good family from Gloucestershire."

From the turn of the stairs Laurence's laugh echoed back to them. "A daughter of the manor house, is she? Blue blood and an icicle under the tongue — I might have guessed."

9

PHILADELPHIA was sorry not to have witnessed the meeting between Laurence Tabor and his uncle's widow, for Mrs. Tabor seemed quite undaunted by this new opponent; his refusal to acknowledge Grace as his long-lost cousin made her highly indignant.

"Would you believe it, Philadelphia, he tried to persuade me that Frank never had a daughter — at least he said I had no proof of it. On the grounds, I suppose, that no one ever told *him*. As though they would, a boy of fourteen! I assured him that I'd had all the facts from Bess Angell. I could see that he was mightily taken aback; the best he could do was to go off muttering that the Angells were all out of their wits, Bess and her brother as well as the rest."

"Why should he say that?"

"Well, my dear, Mr. Angell was a spendthrift, I don't deny. He bought houses and land in all directions, and two ships that were to go trading for gems in the Orient, only they got sunk in a storm off Gravesend. And by this time his debts were so great that the whole family had to leave the City under a cloud. But that's no reason for Laurence to speak slightingly of Bess because she bravely stood by Frank after the scandal. Or to sneer at her brother Tom, who was once his dearest friend."

Laurence's interview with Mrs. Tabor had left him rather thoughtful, and when he next saw Philadelphia, he made her a graceful apology for having tried to provoke her at their first encounter in the shop.

"Think no more of it," she told him with studied calm.

Laurence certainly did not look the part of a city merchant, and she could not imagine what would happen if he wore a pair of skin-tight hose to serve in the shop. It was against the law to wear the clothes of another social class, and though people laughed at the sumptuary laws and broke them quite cheerfully, the Livery Companies were inclined to be strict about these things.

The Downes family made a silent inventory of his clothes at supper, and abused them afterwards.

"Did you see his breeches, Joel? I thought he was going to split them when he sat down." Sam was fourteen; his ideas of humour were primitive.

"He's been to a good tailor," admitted Joel. "Heaven knows what all that gear must have cost him."

"Putting his wages on his back," said their father with a certain gloomy relish. "And the arrogance of it, walking through Cheapside with a sword on his hip . . ."

"I dare say he needed a sword in all those foreign places," said Sam, trying to be fair.

"And his ruff a foot high," continued Mr. Downes. "If he wears such a monstrous erection in the shop . . ."

"You don't suppose he means to work in the shop?" interrupted Joel with a bitter laugh. "That'll be left to us poor menials, while his mightiness sits back and enjoys the profits. Painting his little pictures when the fancy takes him, and apeing the gentry."

And a very ill-judged performance he made of it, thought Philadelphia, who was still nettled by Laurence's comments on her own gentility. (Blue blood and icicle under the tongue, indeed!)

Next morning Mr. Downes and Joel were slightly taken aback when Laurence announced that he wished to make a detailed inspection of the stock. Soberly dressed, with a mere frill at his throat (half-way between a merchant and a gentleman, so to speak) he came down punctually and made his requirements perfectly plain.

"Don't you trust the ledgers?" began Joel, touchy because he thought his father's honesty was being called in question.

"I am not concerned with the ledgers at present. I want to see for myself the exact nature of the stock we are carrying."

So Edmund Beck was left in the front of the house to deal with customers, while Mr. Downes, Joel, Ralph Palmer and the two apprentices got everything off the shelves and out of the iron-bound chests, and set upon the benches in the workshop.

There were cups and mazers, salts and ewers of monumental solidity, every inch of the surface crusted with decoration; plates and spoons; flat, polished chargers and gilt standing dishes, as well as a few exotic trifles, like the coconut cups with their shells rubbed smooth and lustrous, mounted on silver stems. All the plate was beautifully worked and impeccably finished, every item a labour of love. The designs were not original; they had been taken out of one of the standard pattern-books, which contained drawings of every possible type of vessel, as well as suggestions for scrolls and borders, and suitable pictures to be copied in chasing or repouseé work. This was the normal practice, nearly all goldsmiths used a pattern-book, but the one they had been using in John Tabor's workshop must have been around a long time; the pieces it had inspired were curiously old-fashioned, heavy and massive, as plate had been during the early part of the century, with none of that upsurge of subtlety and fantasy which had swept

England into the high Renaissance, at long last, during the past few years.

For instance, there were too many mazers, the deep, wide-mouthed drinking-bowls that had been largely replaced by tall cups and goblets.

Laurence picked up one of them, breathed on it, and rubbed it against his sleeve, for the pleasure of seeing the metal come up more glittering than ever. He followed the delicate chasing of vine-leaves with his thumb.

"Your work, Ralph?"

"Aye, Master Laurence," said the old journeyman, smiling. He was a man of few words; all he thought and felt was told by his hands.

"I thought so. A marvellous example of its kind." Laurence put the bowl down, and asked Zachary, "How many of those have you sold in the last twelve-month?"

"I — I don't precisely recall."

"Why?" demanded Joel, getting ready to be truculent.

"Because people have stopped using mazers."

"Your uncle never believed that. He was convinced that there would always be a market for such good English ware."

"And he made sure that no one contradicted him. Well, so much for the plate; may I now see the jewels?"

Some of the jewellery was old; there seemed to be a good many round hat-brooches of a once popular type, not unlike the religious badges that used to have portraits of the saints on them. There was also a box containing the broken-up fragments of discarderd ornaments, cameos and intaglios, some of them very ancient, as well as loose stone — pearls, lapis lazuli, chalcedony — waiting to be reset. There were some plain gold chains, the sort that measured out a man's status by the number and weight of the links. Apart from these, the new jewellery was tawdry, brittle, inferior stuff, not worthy of the rest of the stock.

Laurence scooped up one of the necklaces that had caught his attention yesterday, and flicked it disdainfully between his fingers.

"What in the name of fortune are you doing with this tin finery? I'm astonished my uncle allowed it in the shop."

"Your uncle didn't like it," admitted Zachary. "He didn't like any of these new-fangled trinkets, but he felt obliged to keep a selection for his customers, and this was the best quality we could come by. I know that it's poor stuff, but what can you expect nowadays, when workmanship is so clumsy, no one takes pride in their craft . . . "

"The work of the continental goldsmiths is finer than it has ever been before."

"This consignment came from the Continent," remarked Joel.

"I was speaking of the designs executed by the greatest masters, not the cheap rubbish that's considered good enough to fob off on the English."

"It may not have occurred to you," retorted Zachary, "that we can't afford to purchase any valuable jewellery. We'd have to tie up too much money, and the profit would be too small."

"I agree. But we could make our own."

Zachary stared at him as though he had gone mad.

"Make our own? Where should we

find the profit in that, pray? A single one of these fantastic new pendants or necklaces would take I don't know how long to complete, and the chances are no one would buy it (for I'm sure I don't know where you'd get your designs) and whatever price we asked, it would be swallowed up by the cost of the materials. When you learn what we have to pay now for gold and gems . . . "

"These new pieces don't depend simply on the value of the stones. The secret is to set them off with a proper use of champlevé enamel."

"Once we start fiddling round with champlevé enamel, we'll never get any work finished," complained Zachary. "I know that kind of time-wasting foolery; you end by botching the whole business, and every scrap has to be melted down again to recover the gold. No, your uncle was right: we should stick to the moulding and casting of plate, as we always have done, and sell a few imported trinkets for what we can get."

"After all," added Joel, "we are smiths by trade. Our whole skill lies in the fashioning of fine silver plate, not in dabbling with paltry little trinkets that look like so many spun sugar sweetmeats."

"My dear Joel, if you can find a way of making jewellery without employing a smith, then you are welcome to call in the pastry-cooks."

The argument raged on. Zachary Downes disapproved of Laurence's suggestion as a matter of course because he disliked any form of change. The idea of making jewellery in their own workshop was new, and the kind that Laurence wanted to make was new also, so both must be condemned.

Joel knew in his heart of hearts that his father, like John Tabor, had been getting steadily more old-fashioned in his outlook, and he had every intention of persuading Zachary into a few innovations, but his impatience was tempered by an aggressive family patriotism. Zachary had borne enough from John Tabor, and Joel wasn't going to stand back and see this idle, jumped-up fellow Laurence setting the place by the ears with his unpractical notions of making a quick profit.

Laurence answered all their objections with an obstinate self-sufficiency that was extremely irritating.

The two apprentices were whispering together by the fire. Sam Downes was the elder, a tough, impudent child with a distinct look of Joel. Will Morris, slighter and more diffident, was his faithful shadow. They were concocting a plan in a volley of suppressed giggles. Unnoticed, they reached down some of the fineing tools that hung over the chimney-breast, went through some form of secret preparation at the furnace, and then, urging each other forward with many thrusts and nudges, they approached the three men who were still talking beside the bench.

"Sir," said Sam to Laurence, "can you settle an argument for us?"

"I'll do my best," said Laurence, smiling.

"Are you a master-goldsmith, like my father?"

The smile vanished. Laurence said, in a cold voice, "When I went abroad, I was a journeyman. I shall have to apply to the Company for the right to call myself a master. Was that the cause of your argument?"

"No, sir — we knew that already," said Sam, with a seraphic innocence. He could see Joel grinning away because the hated usurper had been forced to admit that he was still only a journeyman.

"Well, make haste, boy; what is it you want to ask Mr. Laurence?" demanded Zachary; he was not exactly displeased himself, but he had better manners than his sons and was a good deal more prudent.

"Will is learning to decorate a border — here, hold it up, Will, for Mr. Laurence to see — he wants to work it with the little chasing tool, but I think he ought to use a heavy graver. What do you say?"

Laurence took the fragment of silver and copper alloy; it was a narrow strip that had been sheared off when some large vessel was being cut into shape. On the rather buckled surface Will had managed to scratch a few shaky lines.

"Yes, you need a firm edge here," remarked Laurence.

Sam was standing attentively beside

him, with a selection of instruments on an iron tray. Laurence reached across and picked up the graver, seizing the metal handle with a decisive grasp. His hand lifted so far, then paused in mid-air, while his expression changed from dumb astonishment to excruciating pain and he let the tool fall with a clatter on to the stone floor.

"My God, it's red-hot!"

He put his burnt hand to his mouth, swearing, while the two boys burst out laughing, and Joel joined in, he couldn't help it.

For they all knew what had happened, they all knew the rough and ready joking which had reduced many a small apprentice to tears on his first day in the shop. You heated one of the tools, handle and all, over the open top of the furnace; then you removed it with the tongs, put it down as bait, and sent the newcomer to fetch it . . . How delightful to have caught Laurence with that old trick. He had come lording it back to Goldsmiths' Row, expecting to be confirmed as a master in his own right — and this was the figure he cut in front of the apprentices. Impossible not to laugh.

"That's enough, Joel," said his father. "And as for you two young rogues, I'm ashamed of you. Indeed, I'm sorry for this, Laurence, but they shall each pay the penalty for their bad behaviour."

"No," said Laurence. "Don't punish them on my account. A poor creature I should be if I couldn't endure a laugh at my own expense."

He tried to speak lightly, but he had gone very white, and he winced as he tried to flex the already stiffening fingers of his injured hand. They all stood staring at him. As though he could not bear that silent mixture of pity and contempt, he turned and hurried out of the workshop, up the wide staircase to the second floor, and straight into someone else he did not wish to meet: Mrs. Philadelphia Whitethorn, busily putting away the clean linen.

He pushed past her without speaking, went into his bedchamber and slammed the door. Philadelphia gaped after him. How strange he had looked: not at all like the smooth-tongued young man who had been so much in command of the situation yesterday.

Inside Laurence's room there were various bumps and bags as though he was hunting rapidly and clumsily through his baggage for something he couldn't find. A hard object dropped and rolled across the floor; then there was a sound of cracking and an exclamation, almost a groan of despair.

Philadelphia tapped on the door and went in, without waiting for an answer.

Laurence's stuff had been strewn about the place, and he had apparently been tipping up the cloak-bags and letting their contents fall out on the bed, using only one hand and distributing a good many items on the floor — that accounted for the cracking sound, he had trodden on the ivory box that held his paint-brushes.

"I wondered if there was anything wrong," began Philadelphia. "Oh — your hand!"

"I've got some ointment to put on it, at least I thought I had, but I don't seem able to find it among all this clutter." He gazed around him distractedly.

"We have an excellent remedy for burns; I'll fetch that."

"What happened?" she enquired presently, weaving a neat white parcel round his hand, as though it was a newly-swaddled infant. "Did you pick up the poker by the wrong end?"

"Something just as elementary."

When he told her about it, she was indignant. "But that's barbarous! And you mean to say that young children are subjected to such pain . . ."

"Not as a rule. The metal handle is heated enough to sting a little. Unluckily those young monkeys were too thorough."

"I hope you mean to make matters hot for them in return."

"And make myself more unpopular than I am already?" he said rather bitterly. "No sense in that. I don't think they meant to hurt me, and I wouldn't care except that it's the hand I work with."

If he was unpopular, it was largely his own fault, he had not tried to be conciliating. All the same, Philadelphia did feel a little sorry for him. Seeing his belongings at close quarters she noticed that although he had several very fine doublets and outer garments, his shirts were worn thin with washing and patching, and his other possessions were rather meagre. She thought that perhaps he had found it a hard struggle to make a living these last few years.

There was a stack of papers on the edge of the dressing-chest, and she could see that they were drawings done with a fine brush, not much more than outlines: A girl pinched into a tight stomacher, a child holding a cat, a spray of roses . . .

"Are those your little pictures?"

"Sketches, merely. For proper limning you use parchment; then it's stuck on a playing-card and given a mount that's been specially made to suit the picture. This is the only one I have by me at present."

He unwrapped a silk kerchief. Inside it lay a gold chain with a circular disc displaying the well-known device of a phoenix rising from the flames. The design was worked in coloured enamels, enriched with rubies and diamonds. When it was reversed, the pendant turned out to be a locket containing the portrait of a young man in riding-dress crisply painted in minute detail.

115

Above his head there was a shield with the inscription: 'W.B. 1589 aet. 26' and a hand holding a flaming torch.

Philadelphia exclaimed with delight. She had not imagined that a miniature could be such a complete and perfect work of art, and she was impressed by Laurence's skill.

"Who is the man in the picture?"

"Walter Brand, a young English gentleman I met on the Continent. He left before the picture was framed, so I promised to bring it home for him. My dear Mrs. Whitethorn, whatever are you doing now?"

"Picking up some of the things you dropped. No, don't complain. It's difficult for you to manage with one arm, and you must know I am your aunt's housekeeper, I'm sure this is one of my duties."

She was still arranging the room, with a brisk composure, when Joel arrived, belatedly. He was surprised to find Philadelphia in Laurence's bedchamber, but had sufficient poise not to say so.

"I hope your hand is not too painful," he began stiffly.

"It will soon mend. In the meantime

116

I am being well taken care of, as you see."

"I did not mean to laugh at your misfortune," pursued Joel, as though reciting a set speech. "I — we did not understand that the burn was so severe."

"Of course not," said Laurence agreeably. "You naturally assumed that I was making much ado about nothing."

Joel looked as though he was going to wreck his careful apology with an outburst of plain speaking, and Philadelphia thought it wise to intervene.

"Mr. Tabor has been showing me one of his miniature pictures."

She thought Joel was bound to admire Laurence's talent as a draughtsman, and hope (perhaps foolishly) that this might make a bond between them. But Joel inspected the portrait and some of the sketches without comment, and then turned the locket over, remarking pointedly that the case was a piece of excellent craftsmanship.

"The work of one of your foreign jewellers, I suppose?"

"It was made in Germany," said

Laurence. He picked up the miniature and wrapped it away in the kerchief.

"You weren't very civil about his painting," Philadelphia told Joel later. "It was very well done, and I think he would have liked you to say so."

"He may be paying my wages, he can't hire my tongue. If he wants admirers, he'll have to look elsewhere. He's a vain, trifling fellow, and I see nothing in him to earn the respect of a working goldsmith."

10

"I CAN'T make out why you want to ask my poor lamb any further questions," Mrs. Tabor complained to her nephew in the gentle, anxious voice with which she had been repeating much the same statement for the past hour.

Her poor lamb sat beside her, head dutifully bent over a piece of embroidery. Laurence stood in front of the fireplace, his arm in a sling, trying to suppress his exasperation.

"It's a matter of collecting evidence, madam. There's no need for Grace to be so much afraid of me. I'm not an ogre."

"Grace is inclined to be timid, which I understand, for I suffer from the same weakness. Frank was very stout-hearted, like the rest of you Tabors, but Grace takes after me."

Mrs. Tabor now called the foundling Grace, to distinguish her from the original Frances, but she insisted on the relationship between them, even when everyone else was trying to examine the facts impartially. She informed Laurence that she meant to remain in the room while he talked to his cousin, and that would make them all quite comfortable.

Laurence was plainly at the end of his tether. It would never be possible to settle Grace's identity, one way or the other, if Mrs. Tabor was going to prompt all her answers.

Philadelphia took pity on him by reminding her mistress that she was expecting a visit from one of her married nieces.

"But if you will let me stay with Grace while Mr. Tabor discusses these matters with her, I hope everyone will be satisfied."

Laurence and Grace were both grateful for this suggestion, and so it was that Philadelphia found herself holding a watching brief in what appeared to be a contest between two very unequal opponents.

They had moved into the parlour, which was at the back of the house, looking out towards Watling Street, with a sideways view of St. Paul's. There was a small courtyard behind the house, and a patch of grass where a few green daffodil spears were thrusting out their yellow tips in the pale March sunlight. Laurence sat at one side of the table, a sheet of foolscap in front of him, making notes awkwardly with his left hand. Grace sat facing him, dumb with apprehension, her fingers gripped tightly together in her lap.

His first question went right back to the roots.

"What is the earliest memory you can recall?"

Grace cleared her throat, nervously. "I fell and cut my leg," she whispered.

"Where?"

"If it please you, sir, I think it was above the knee."

Laurence took a deep breath. "The place where this happened; can you remember that?"

Grace thought it was at a cottage in the country, near a pond. She had closed her eyes while she was speaking, as though dredging up images from inside her brain. Philadelphia thought that it would be a clever way of protecting herself, if she was lying, from the scrutiny of the man opposite.

The inquisition continued. Some of his questions she could not answer. Some of her memories might have come out of anyone's early youth. Where she mentioned details that coincided with the known history of little Frances Tabor, Philadelphia found her credible and consistent.

Laurence pushed back his chair. "Very well, I've done asking you questions. But let me tell you this. If you have been drawn into a wicked plot by others or forced to impersonate my cousin against your conscience, then I advise you to confess the truth straight away, and I promise you shall not be punished. But if you are telling deliberate lies, and go on lying for your own advancement, I warn you that we shall catch you in the end, and you'll get no mercy from any of us."

Philadelphia expected an outburst from Grace after this harsh pronouncement, but Grace just sat there supine, staring towards Laurence in an unfocused way, like a bird spellbound by a snake. Then she asked, "May I go now?" scrambled to her feet and fled from the room.

"Was there any need to be so brutal?" asked Philadelphia, her voice stiff with disapproval.

"I hoped I might persuade her to admit her guilt openly, before she is found out."

"What makes you so sure she is guilty? Hasn't it occurred to you, Mr. Tabor, that the child cannot know for certain whether she is your cousin or not?"

"Yes it has occurred to me. I think she knows more than you bargain for, but I am willing to hold my hand until I get some further proof."

He was strangely determined not to allow for the faintest possibility that Grace might be his cousin; Philadelphia wondered why. Perhaps one fortune wasn't enough for him? Having come into everything his uncle had to leave, he might regard himself as the proper person to inherit the fairly large slice of the estate which had been settled on his aunt. This suggested an ugly, insatiable greed, not quite in keeping with the young man who had gone off to live as a wandering painter on the Continent rather than submit to the tyranny of his rich uncle. She thought it possible that his chief grudge against Grace was the fact that she was sponsored by the Downes family.

While she was trying to take Laurence's measure, he had apparently been taking hers.

"Why are you so anxious to support this girl?" he demanded. "What's your interest in the matter?"

"I have none." This was not entirely true. She had several shadowy motives, strengthened by a desire to see him put in the wrong. However, she had no personal axe to grind, so it was easy to look virtuous, and say, "I simply wish for the truth to prevail."

"And I suppose you think that the conception of blind justice means walking around with your eyes shut?"

"No, I don't!" she snapped. "I fancy I can see as far as you, and in any case, I'd sooner have blind justice than blind prejudice. It's no concern of mine, but I should say you would be very unwise to let your disagreements in the shop colour your whole outlook."

Laurence studied her dispassionately. "You are right in one particular, Mrs. Whitethorn."

"I'm glad to hear you say so. Which one?"

"That it's no concern of yours."

11

GRACE was frightened.

She loitered on the top floor, keeping out of everyone's way and trying to wrestle with her fears while she waited for Joel. Luckily it was easy to stay out of sight; the space and privacy at Goldsmiths' Row was one of the things that had astonished her most, after the continual public exposure of life at the Charity Hospital. Ownership and isolation had given her a separateness that she had never been able to acquire until now, and after a taste of this special kind of liberty, as well as the many other advantages it would be a dreadful fate to be banished from Goldsmiths' Row.

But this wasn't the reason she had kept her mouth shut when Mr. Laurence urged her to confess. She wasn't greedy or over-confident, she simply hadn't the courage to tell the truth. Mr. Laurence had said she wouldn't be punished if she spoke up at once, and she took this to

126

mean that the Tabors themselves would not have her put in prison, but since she would no longer have any claim on them, she supposed they would send her back to the Charity Hospital. And Mr. Silas Tucker would have to be told why.

Grace sat on the top stair in the growing dusk, gazing down through a basketwork pattern of receding banister rails to a lighted triangle of the stone-flagged hall, four flights below. It was very quiet up here, the maids were all in the kitchen. She had left a message for Joel with his brother Sam; she had found it easy to make friends with the apprentices, who reminded her of the boys at the Charity Hospital.

Presently there was the small tongue of a candle-flame climbing up towards her, and Joel's voice, grumbling but a little amused.

"What are you skulking up here in the dark for, you silly girl? There's nothing wrong, is there?"

"Oh yes there is," she assured him earnestly. "Mr. Laurence has been questioning me for hours, the same things over and over again, and he doesn't believe a word I say, he told me I must confess my guilt at once or they'd show me no mercy, and I'm sure he means to go to the Charity Hospital and find out the truth. They'll give me back to Mr. Tucker, and he'll just about kill me for being so wicked. I can't bear to think of what he'll do to me."

The words poured out at a gathering speed and panic. Joel sat down on the stair beside her, and put an arm round her thin shoulders.

"Now stop making that abominable noise, do you hear me? I've been to Southwark this afternoon. Laurence'll get no satisfaction at the Charity Hospital."

"Joel! What did you do?"

"I saw Mrs. Bullace — who was glad to get such good reports of you, by the way. I asked her if there was not a book recording the names of all the orphans and the dates they came to the Hospital; she told me that the book they are using at present is no more than six years old; there was a previous book, with your name in it, but this was burnt in a fire you had at the Hospital last Michaelmas twelve-month."

"Was it?" said Grace, rather surprised. "I knew that some clothes and blankets were destroyed, but I didn't think any books — Oh! I see! You mean that Mrs. Bullace has got rid of the book, and she told Mr. Tucker it went in the fire?"

"Yes, and providentially she had the wit to do so very soon after you came here. So if Laurence goes to Southwark and asks to see the records, Tucker will have no hesitation in telling him that they went up in smoke. And then you will be perfectly safe; they won't find a note of your admission as a babe in arms in 'seventy-four, and they won't find the date in 'seventy-nine when Frances Tabor ought to have arrived on the doorstep. Both those years are in the book that's vanished, and the only account of your coming to the Hospital is to be had from Mrs. Bullace. She won't fail us, never fear, and no one can gainsay her."

"Mrs. Bullace always knows what's best," said Grace, much more placidly.

"I'm sure she does. So why were you in such dire straits, carrying on as though you were bound for Tyburn?"

"I was very stupid. Only I can't understand why Mr. Laurence is so certain that I'm not his cousin. I must have done something to make him suspicious, and I wish I knew what it was."

"It's nothing to do with you, my dear. I'm the one he mistrusts; he'd be bound to suspect any heiress that I rescued out of a home for pauper foundlings. In fact I doubt if he believes you were ever inside the place at all, so he's going to get a rap on the knuckles for his evil-thinking when he meets Mrs. Bullace and Mr. Tucker."

"Doesn't think I was at the Charity Hospital!" echoed Grace. "Where else would I have come from?"

"He probably takes it for granted that you're my doxy."

Grace gave a small gasp of astonishment. "You've no cause to look so scandalised," said Joel, laughing at the perplexed face he could just see in the candle-light. "I wish it was true. I should enjoy having such a pretty companion in my bed."

He gave her a tentative, glancing kiss on the side of the mouth, while he began to caress her almost absent-mindedly, pinching her plump little breasts through the stuff of her dress.

She jerked herself away from him, outraged and protesting.

"Joel, you must not — I cannot — please, Joel, let me alone."

"Very well, I won't tease you." Quickly recognising that he had made a false move, he released her and adopted the manner of an elder brother. "You must try not to be so fearful, always looking on the dark side at every shift of fortune. Let Laurence go to Southwark; it won't do you a mite of harm, you'll see."

And he was right. Laurence went over to the Charity Hospital, but had nothing to say on the subject when he got back, and showed no signs of wanting to ask Grace any more questions. He might not be satisfied that she was the rightful claimant — one day the following week he rode out to Enfield, which Joel found very amusing. As he pointed out to Grace, it didn't matter how much anyone searched for discrepancies in the early history of Frances Tabor's daughter. He himself would be vindicated at every stage.

12

LAURENCE still insisted that he wasn't yet able to use the heavy tools in the workshop. His right hand was still tender and there had been some festering under the scar.

"Did you ever meet such a glib fellow?" commented Joel. "He can certainly make excuses, if he can't make anything else."

In spite of his disability, Laurence applied to the Company for recognition as a master-goldsmith, and this was granted immediately. Joel, of course, was furious. He said it was monstrously unjust that members of important and wealthy families were allowed to advance in the Company without passing the tests which were set for ordinary mortals.

Laurence soon found that he was able to start painting again; the fine, thin brushes — pencils, he called them — with which he drew and coloured his little pictures were much easier to hold than the goldsmith's mallets and chasers.

He went to call on Walter Brand, the young man whose miniature he had painted in Germany and brought home with him. Brand visited Goldsmiths' Row; he was a lively and entertaining young man with no starchy pride about him. Grace had never observed a proper gentleman at close quarters before and was slightly disappointed.

"Why he's no grander than Mr. Laurence!" she said.

This annoyed Joel and made Philadelphia laugh.

Mrs. Tabor had decided that she would like Laurence to paint Grace, and might have made an issue of it, if Grace had not been so extremely reluctant. She was sure he would not want to paint her and if he agreed, merely to please his aunt, it would be even worse, because in drawing her features he would be bound to penetrate her secret — she regarded his gifts with a superstitious awe. She begged so earnestly to be let off that Mrs. Tabor said he had better do a portrait of her niece Judith Beck instead.

After a shuffle of sleeping quarters, Laurence had acquired the second-best

133

bedchamber which had once belonged to Mr. Zachary Downes. He kept his painting things up there. It was unthinkable that Laurence should be closeted in his bedchamber alone with Judith Beck, who was a very well brought-up girl, like all Hannah's daughters, and while she was with him it was arranged that Philadelphia should keep them company. Sometimes Grace went with her, a silent and wondering spectator.

Judith sat on a stool by the window, the light of an April morning falling on her good, calm face. Her corn-coloured hair was not so fair as Grace's, but it was thick and heavy, falling to her waist. Laurence stood a few feet away from her, working meticulously at a small square of parchment that was propped on the table and surrounded by beakers of paint. He stared and squinted and measured with his thumb, occasionally inspecting Judith with such an unflattering scowl that Grace wondered how she could bear it. But Judith seemed entirely self-possessed.

"Are you going to put in some kind of symbolic conceit?" she asked on one occasion.

"Mind what you are about, Mrs. Judith," said Walter Brand, who had looked in to see how the picture was progressing. "These limners are terrible fellows, they paint whatever comes into their heads, and the next thing you know you'll be sharing your portrait with a cabbage or a caterpillar!"

"You do talk the most unmitigated nonsense," said Laurence cheerfully. "Pay no attention to him, Judith. There won't be any caterpillars, I promise."

It was true that most of his portraits had some sort of mysterious addition. One of the finished pictures was leaning on the oak shelf above the chimney, as well as two others that were not yet complete. Laurence liked to arrange his people in sharp outline against a background of warm terracotta (just as Nicholas Hilliard always used blue, so Philadelphia said). Grace knew nothing about Nicholas Hilliard, but she was sure that nobody could make these little manikins more real, with their faces so still yet so lifelike, and their clothes so exquisitely copied that you could recognise the material, lawn or velvet

135

or lace, and even guess what stitches had been used in the embroidery. The sitter's initials were generally inscribed, and then there were the fantastic conceits; one lady was holding a little rose-tree with a heart in the middle of it, and there was a young man with a sun and moon behind his head.

"What do such devices mean?" asked Philadelphia. "Are they a play on words, on the names of the sitters?"

"Names or pet-names, references to the names of their lovers, or to the state of their feelings. I am often asked to convey a message which can be read only by the recipient, the person for whom the picture is painted. That's the whole purpose of the limner's art," said Laurence, thoughtfully contemplating the lady with the rose tree. "Full-sized portraits are hung on the wall for everyone to see. But the little pictures that a limner makes are meant to be treasured and admired in private, or shown to a few chosen friends. Even when they are mounted in lockets, we are at pains to design a beautiful case, so that they can be worn with the reverse side outwards. A limner is like a sonnet-writer, they are both creating images for the delectation of an intimate circle, not trying to satisfy the curiosity of strangers." He paused. "Shall I give you an example, Mrs. Whitethorn? I know what device I should use if I was painting you."

Philadelphia flushed. "I can't imagine I should ever be fool enough to sit for you."

He seized on a fresh sheet of paper, brushed a few lines across it and handed it to her. She took one glance, screwed up the paper and threw it on to the hearth. Then she returned to her sewing, with a face of stone. Laurence said nothing and went on working at his portrait of Judith.

Grace was longing to know what he had put on the paper that Philadelphia found so offensive. Presently she managed to retrieve it from the brick floor of the unlit fire and surreptitiously smoothed out the creases.

He had made a vivid little sketch, the strokes were so fine he might have been using a needle. In it, Philadelphia was blindfolded and holding a tiny pair of scales that were steeply dipped at one end. Grace did not understand what this was supposed to convey, but she could see what had upset Philadelphia. In drawing an imaginary bandage for her eyes, he had let it run upwards to cover the place on her forehead that was pitted with smallpox.

She did not know whether he had been careless or deliberately cruel, she did not know very much about men and how their mind worked; she understood Philadelphia a good deal better, for one thing she had learnt at the Charity Hospital was that a great many people had some burden of ugliness or weakness or stupidity which they themselves never forgot, even when it had become accepted and taken for granted. She suspected that Philadelphia's smallpox scars were just such a burden.

On a fine April morning soon after Easter Grace accompanied Mrs. Tabor to market. They crossed the hurly-burly of Cheapside to the place Philadelphia called 'the land of milk and honey', because the main supply of fresh food from the country villages was offered for sale at the booths and little shops clustered around Milk Street and Honey Lane.

Mrs. Tabor did not come over here often, she left the marketing to Philadelphia, but this morning she wanted to find a particular farmer's wife whom she had dealt with for many years, so that they could be sure of a good supply of gooseberries and strawberries early in the summer. She was soon engaged in a pleasant gossip with Goodwife Salter, while Grace stood behind her letting the sights and sounds and scents of Cheapside wash over her in waves.

The lowing of a cow that was being milked in the street, the freckles on the milkmaid's fat elbows . . . A mouthwatering smell of hot mutton pies . . . Other smells, less fragrant: people tramping by with dung and straw on their boots . . . Two little girls who had come in from the country with their mother; they had a flat basket full of primroses, done up in posies.

She did not see the sandy-haired boy in the shabby jerkin until he stopped and spoke her name. Then she turned and gave a squeak of pleasure. It was Coney from the Charity Hospital.

They gazed at each other, almost unable to speak. Though they had been living only a few miles apart, they were so much at the mercy of other people's whims that they had hardly expected to meet again.

"I reckon you've grown into a regular fine lady, Grace," he said at last and with a hint of disapproval.

"Oh no!" she protested, flushing. She felt awkward for a good many reasons, the chief one being that Coney knew how little right she had to go peacocking around in her splendid new clothes.

"What are you doing in this part of London?" she asked, to change the subject.

"Haven't I as much right here as you?"

He hadn't forgiven her for going to Goldsmiths' Row or for the lies she had told in order to get there. It was easy for him, he was by nature so honest and proud, not to say tough; he seemed taller than she remembered, and his shoulders were broader than ever;

140

he was bursting out of his threadbare coat and breeches, which were white with the ground-in-dust of the mason's yard. And he didn't care a bit about his shabby clothes, he looked as pleased with himself as if he owned the whole street, and his bad temper disappeared under a sudden smile, because he couldn't resist the impulse to tell her a piece of good news.

"Do you truly want to know why I'm here? You know my master, Melchior Breda, was a famous carver of monuments in the Netherlands, before he came to England? Now at last he has found a patron, and he's been chosen to devise the tomb of a rich merchant in that church there — St. Mary Magdalen, Milk Street. It will take months to complete, and because of this, my master has more money to spare. He's moved into a better lodging, and I live there with him, to keep the place clean and cook his meals. So I am free of the Charity Hospital too."

"Coney, I am so glad!"

She could understand, better than anyone, how much it meant to him to escape from the imprisoning walls of the Charity Hospital, where they were all drilled into uniformity like so many peas in a pod, and instead to be a unique person in his own right. His circumstances were very modest, but that didn't matter. He was delighted with his corner by the fire, his truckle-bed under the stairs, and the right to spend a holiday hanging around the boats on the river, on the chance that one of the watermen might give him a free trip, or going to the shooting-fields at Clerkenwell, where he could learn to use the long bow. London was his oyster.

"You should have been to see me," said Grace. "It's only just across the way."

Coney's pleasure was clouded over. "I did come," he said, shuffling his feet. "They told me to get out and stay out."

"What? Who could have done such a thing? They can't have understood properly. Madam!" She turned impulsively to Mrs. Tabor, who had just finished her chat with the farmer's wife. "Madam, this is Coney that was at the Charity Hospital, he's my great friend, he's always taken care of me, and he says he came to visit me, but one of the men, I suppose it was Mr. Zachary, told him to go away. And they never even gave me the message!"

"Well, my dear, it's very unfortunate," said Mrs. Tabor, beginning to twitter and eyeing Coney with a mixture of annoyance and apprehension. "I hoped you wouldn't find out. I was afraid you would be distressed . . . "

"Madam, do you mean to say that *you* made them send him away?"

"Hush, Grace. People are beginning to stare. As for you, young man, you've no business to pester my grand-daughter . . . "

"He wasn't pestering me!"

Mrs. Tabor embarked on a rambling appeal to Coney. "You must know that you would be in serious trouble if I was to complain — not that I ever should, if it's true that you were kind to her in that horrible place — even so, that's over now, you are neither of you children any more, and you belong to quite a different state of life; surely you must see that it's not fitting?"

While she spoke, Mrs. Tabor had been tugging at the strings of her purse; at last she got them disentangled, dived in and brought up two large silver coins, which she held out to Coney.

"Here, boy. Here's for your disappointment."

Until then, Coney had been standing his ground, not much impressed by anything Mrs. Tabor had to say. Now he backed away from her, red in the face and furious.

"Keep your dirty money, I want none of it. I may not be good enough for the likes of you, but at least I never tried to reach a state of life where I don't belong."

He stalked off up Milk Street, and disappeared through the side door of the church.

13

MRS. TABOR and Grace were flurried and disturbed by their encounter with Coney; Philadelphia had to calm them both.

"They are each feeling ill-used by the other," she informed Joel. "They are so extremely alike; if I still doubted Grace's claims, I should be convinced by the way she takes after her grandmother."

"Would you?" said Joel, hugging his secret triumph. Given enough audacity, you could make people believe anything.

"Poor Grace is so fond of the boy that she very nearly said she wanted to go back to the Charity Hospital."

"I hope she's not such a fool," said Joel sharply.

"I don't think there is any inducement strong enough to make her return willingly into the power of that monster Tucker. Besides, the boy himself is no longer boarding at the Hospital, she wouldn't see him if she did go. She'll

145

forget him as soon as she can make some new friends of her own age; it's a pity we can't go to the Goldsmiths' banquet this year, but it wouldn't be seemly, Mrs. Tabor being so recent a widow."

The banquet was an annual event, all that was left of the religious festival of Catholic times, when the members of the ancient Guild had celebrated the feast of their patron St. Dunstan by going to Mass together in solemn procession.

"And we ought to venerate him still," grumbled Ralph. "A proper English saint, Dunstan was, not like some of those papish foreigners, and a brother craftsman to boot. It's well known he used a pair of goldsmith's tongs when he caught the devil by the nose."

"You'd better take care how you dabble in theology," said Laurence, "or one of the devil's representatives will get you by the nose. There are too many of them about, disguised as puritan ministers."

Laurence was going to the banquet; no question of his staying at home to mourn his uncle. Probably Philadelphia and Grace could have gone too if he had cared to ask the wife of one of the liverymen to take them under her wing. But he wouldn't do that, because it would have been a tacit admission that he accepted Grace as his cousin.

The banquet took place at midday in the Goldsmiths' Hall; there was a high table across the top of the room, where the master-craftsmen sat, among them Sir Richard Martin, the reigning Lord Mayor, and his Sheriffs, Hugh Offley and Richard Saltenstall, all three of them being goldsmiths. There was always an impressive display of civic scarlet and badges of office at the high table, alternating with the coloured hoods of the Liverymen. The journeymen sat at two long trestles which ran down the middle of the hall, while the female guests — the merchants' wives and daughters — sat at separate tables near the wall.

Along the centre of every table stood the ceremonial plate; salts, bowls and chargers, richly embossed and engraved, polished to the smoothness of glass and glittering with light. The Queen herself had nothing to surpass the treasures which generations of goldsmiths had presented to their own Company.

From his rather lowly seat among the journeymen, Joel could see his father, at the end of the masters' table, eating his dinner and talking quietly to one old crony; he always remained in the background, in the shadows, had no ambition to take a leading part in the affairs of the Company. Joel watched him with an irritable affection. The old man would never set the Thames on fire, but he'd had a hard life and many disappointments; he hadn't come into an undeserved fortune at the age of twenty-nine, just for being the nephew of a rich man who wanted to perpetuate a famous name. There had been an unbroken line of Tabors among the master-craftsmen for nearly three centuries; that was why those revered grey bears welcomed Laurence so complacently. He was looking very fine today, with his uncle's heaviest gold chain wreathed across his shoulders, and a long, brocaded gown whose fur-lined sleeves fell open from the elbow; his hair lay thick and smooth under his flat cap, and he smelt like a barber's shop, thought

Joel contemptuously. He was certainly the main topic of interest among the women. As Joel glanced in their direction, he caught the eye of a girl called Audrey Freeman, who had been his companion at most of the Christmas festivities a few weeks before John Tabor's death, when everyone thought that Zachary Downes was about to become his partner. The way Audrey had behaved with him at the Twelfth Night revels you would have thought she could hardly wait to have the banns called, but today she returned his smile with a stare of brazen indifference. They were all the same, those merchants' daughters, ready to romp in the dark so long as their parents didn't find out, but when it came to marriage they were cold-blooded and purse-proud, with an absurd notion of their own value. Not one of them could hold a candle to Grace. As he considered this, a splendid new plan shaped itself completely in his mind.

He would marry Grace.

He could not imagine why he had never thought of this before. He had plunged with her into a reckless game of false pretences because he wanted money, and also because he wanted revenge, and saddling the Tabor family with the child of a Bankside harlot was a very good joke, even if he couldn't share it. His revenge still amused him; as for the money, so far he had received only a fraction of the reward, and some of that he had passed on to Mrs. Bullace; it was important to keep her happy. That devil Laurence had got the attorney to persuade Mrs. Tabor that she shouldn't give him any more until Grace's identity was proved, one way or the other. Which it never would be. Joel felt sure he would get the whole sum in the end — the old woman was already convinced — but the most generous reward would not be enough to set him and his father up in a shop of their own, and buy back Sam's indentures from Laurence, so that they could take him with them. Grace's dowry, however, would be a different matter.

In the ordinary way Joel knew he would not be considered a suitable match for an heiress; his family and prospects were too insignificant; his hopes depended on the fact that Grace might not get the sort of offers Mrs. Tabor was probably counting on. The great City dynasties were cautious about whose blood they mixed in their veins; it was not Grace's illegitimacy they would cavil at, but the fear that she might not be a Tabor at all, even on the wrong side of the blanket. If Mrs. Tabor was given time to realise this, wouldn't she be thankful to settle for a less exacting member of the Company who merely needed a nest-egg to start him on his way to fame and fortune? After all, he'd rescued Grace from a life of bondage, hadn't he? They would do very well with a shop on Lombard Street and if Grace was rather stupid, she was very pretty and also industrious and obedient; he wouldn't have any trouble making a dutiful wife out of her. He indulged his fancy as he went on eating and drinking this way through everything that was put in front of him.

"You're very quiet," said his neighbour. "Still brooding over the iniquity of Laurence Tabor? I can't see what's wrong with the fellow."

Joel's grievance had become a favourite jest among his fellow-lodgers in Bachelors'

Alley. This riled him, and he flushed angrily.

"He's a man of straw, that's what's wrong with him. A braggart and a pretender, crying his wares in the front of the shop, but when it comes to an honest day's work at the furnace, you won't see hair nor hide of him. Oh, I grant you he can prick out his little pictures as finely as a gentlewoman sewing seams, but that's not the proper employment of a master-goldsmith. Eight weeks and more he's been back in London, and all he's done, besides these paltry limnings, is to fiddle around with some trifling pins and gilded wire. Not a piece of regular smith's work have we seen."

"No," said Edmund Beck, "because he injured his right hand — through a trick that was played by your brother."

Joel tried to get up, which was difficult because the bench was pushed in too near the table. "Are you insinuating . . . "

"Oh, for heaven's sake, Joel, sit still. You're making a song and dance about nothing."

Joel was dimly aware of this, and he was not sorry to be interrupted by the

Master of Ceremonies striking the board with his mace, a sign that he was about to propose the Queen's health. They finally emerged from the banqueting hall in the middle of the afternoon, and Joel spent the rest of the holiday rollicking round the taverns with a host of boon companions. As time went by, he knew less and less about what was happening. There was drink and laughter and lewd stories and someone falling down. (Someone? It was me, he decided painfully.) There was more drink, and pushing and shouting in the dark streets, and some sort of scuffle with the watch. Another fall, into the stinking gutter this time, and then he was being dragged up a flight of stairs and dumped on the floor of his lodging in Bachelors' Alley — a floor that pitched up and down under him all night long, like a ship in a heavy sea.

One of his friends roused him next morning with heartless exhortations and a wet towel; the squalid room was still swaying slightly, and he felt stiff, crumpled and extremely ill. But there was no help for it, he had somehow to dress himself properly and go to work.

He arrived late in Goldsmiths' Row, with a parchment complexion and stabs of flame burning through his eyeballs, to be met by an impatient Laurence, who said, "We've been waiting for you this half-hour. Wasn't the night long enough for you?"

"I overslept," mumbled Joel, wondering resentfully how Laurence managed to look so spruce this morning. He had certainly drunk deep enough yesterday, yet here he was saying that he always woke early after a feast. Life was very unjust.

Laurence had been inspired to start working on a commission he had been given by one of his uncle's best customers. For the last week or so, since his hand had finally healed, he had been finicking with some little trifles of jewellery, but this morning he had decided to begin making the flat silver dish that was to be encircled with a wreath of laurels and inscribed with a famous coat of arms.

"And I shall need you and Ralph to help me at the forge," he announced carelessly.

Joel's heart sank. The mere mention

of the forge oppressed his spirits. When you wanted to hammer metal into a particular shape you had to soften it in the furnace, and then beat it on the anvil. The important thing was to work as fast as possible, while it was still pliable, so in the case of a large piece like a charger it was usual for three men to work at the anvil together. But did he have to be one of them? He asked hopefully where Edmund was. Laurence had sent Edmund round to the assay-master with some plate that needed the Company's hall-mark, and Sam had gone with him. Apart from Laurence and Ralph, that left Joel's father, who was in the shop, and the younger apprentice Will, who was busy pumping at the organ-bellows. Joel knew that he couldn't cry off while there was no one to take his place except an old man and a small boy. Crossly, he tugged at the points of his doublet, while Laurence put the silver bullion into an iron cradle that was slung above the pinkish-white, incandescent fire.

At least, Joel thought sourly, this comedy was not likely to continue long, for Laurence must be woefully out of practice. No doubt he wanted to pretend that he was making an important piece of plate, but it was Ralph who would do the work.

Presently Laurence brought over the great lump of silver in a shovel, and dipped it into a bucket of cold water. The water spluttered and a jet of steam hissed upwards to the ceiling. Laurence fished out the sluggish, yielding metal, placed it on the anvil, holding it steady with a pair of tongs, and the three men began to flatten it. Their hammer blows fell in a steady rhythm. First Laurence's, then Ralph's, then Joel's: chink — chink — chink. Joel was sweating. It was a warm, overcast morning, and the workshop was stifling from the heat of the furnace. He began to breathe quicker, and glanced at Laurence out of the corner of his eye to see how he was bearing the strains. Laurence seemed perfectly happy; he was hitting the target firm and true every time. Joel gritted his teeth and struggled to keep pace with his two companions, though the shock of each blow came shivering up his arms, through the back of his neck and into his throbbing head.

At last there was a respite. The now flattened block of silver had hardened with beating, as it always did, and needed to be freshly annealed at the fire. this time Ralph took it over there. Laurence waited, resting one foot on the base of the anvil, and playing idly with his mallet. He looked a great deal tougher in his shirt-sleeves than Joel had expected, and was evidently as strong as a horse in spite of his slim build. He used his body with a supple economy of movement which brought one fact home to Joel with an astonishing certainty: this wasn't a man who had done nothing more active for the last six years than paint little pictures. Whatever else he had done on the continent, Laurence must have spent a good deal of his time as a working goldsmith.

He ought to have told us, thought Joel indignantly. And then remembered that they hadn't wanted to listen.

All too soon the turgid grey lump was back on the anvil and they were hammering it once more. Joel's fingers kept slipping down the handle of his mallet; twice he botched his stroke altogether. There was a pain in his chest and his mouth was as dry as a sandpit.

When Laurence next called a halt, Joel half hoped that he or Ralph would see to the annealing. He waited, pressing his hands over his eyes.

"Get on, man," Laurence ordered him. "It's your turn at the fire."

He had to go through the whole process, carefully watching the battered chunk of silver and copper alloy until the surface liquefied to exactly the right consistency. The temperature near the furnace was intolerable. He staggered back with the shovel of hot silver and nearly lost it in the bucket. By the time he got it squarely on the anvil he would have given anything for a rest and a cool drink. Instead he had to take up his mallet immediately, though he was scarcely able to swing it; he had a stitch in his side and he felt sick, and the scene kept wavering before him and floating away into a black swamp. Though he could see so little, he always managed to see Laurence's face; taut, hostile and contemptuous. Ralph was there too, keeping his place in the orderly rotation, yet he was no longer aware of Ralph. He was involved in a fantastic duel with Laurence, and he was losing.

The swamp engulfed him; he had to beg for mercy.

"For God's sake — I can't . . . "

His mallet went crashing on to the stone floor. Then someone put an arm round him and steering him out into the yard at the back of the house. He slumped there, gulping, doubled over with faintness and nausea, until his vision cleared and he discovered that the person supporting him was Laurence.

This effected a rapid cure. Making a great effort, he managed to stand upright.

"Take it slowly, you'll soon recover," said Laurence, not unkindly.

"I'm well enough." He felt it necessary to make some kind of apology. "The truth is, I drank too much yesterday."

"You were in good company."

But they didn't all make such damned fools of themselves, thought Joel, brooding. It had started to drizzle, and both young men welcomed the cool rain that trickled down their necks and soaked through their thin shirts.

"How many demonstrations will you require before you are satisfied?" added Laurence.

"Satisfied — in what respect?"

"That I am fit to occupy the place of a master-goldsmith and to employ craftsmen of your quality. Come now, Joel, there's no sense in putting on those airs of innocence; these are the claims you've been refusing to accept since the day I came home. And I'm damned if I can see why; I may not be as good as my uncle or your father in their heyday, but I was their pupil, as you very well know; I was a journeyman of about your standing when you were serving your indentures, and if you have forgotten how my uncle dealt with idleness or bad workmanship, I certainly haven't. He thought my painting was a sinful waste of time, and when I refused to give it up, he turned me out of doors — but no one gave you leave to suppose that I paint portraits because I'm too stupid to do anything else. Limners don't earn much, as a rule, and I should have had a lean time these past six years if I'd not had a second trade at my finger-tips and the sense of profit by what I could learn from foreign masters. Remember that, next time you feel tempted to treat me as an unskilled ignoramus."

Joel muttered something incoherent. He was too confused to defend himself, and indeed he hadn't much of a defence. He could first recall Laurence at the age of twenty, already fighting a continual battle with his uncle because he wanted to be a painter. With a little encouragement Joel might have been inclined to take his side, but there had been nothing very heroic about this rebel, white-faced and sullen, hunched over his little chalk scribbles and repelling any sort of friendly curiosity with that sharp tongue of his. It only dawned on him now that Laurence must have been desperately unhappy; the boy Joel could not have envisaged that sort of unhappiness. Instead, he had accepted the popular opinion, which was not that Laurence was trying to escape from the shop because he wanted to paint, but that he wanted to paint because he was a poor craftsman who did not like working at the forge. That was old John Tabor, twisting the truth, damn him. Because of his insidious prejudice, Joel had grown up thinking of Laurence as a weak, pretentious idler unequal to the rigorous virility of the goldsmith's craft. And then John Tabor had fooled him again with that monstrous will, cutting out the Downes family and leaving everything to the nephew he had taught them to despise. It was a wicked injustice — but all at once began to see Laurence as another of the old man's victims.

"I'm sorry," he managed at last, "if I've seemed uncivil. I never thought of you as — well, we none of us did. We've all been misled!"

"Misled?" repeated Laurence. He spoke lightly, but Joel thought there was a dangerous under-current in his voice. "I dare say. I never knew a houseful of people who'd got hold of the wrong end of so many sticks. If you have any more trifling misapprehensions to clear up, I am perfectly willing to listen. But I warn you, Joel, I may not always feel so magnanimous."

"No," said Joel loudly, blustering a little. "There's nothing else. What should there be?"

Laurence turned and went back into the workshop.

14

TOWARDS the end of June, Mrs. Tabor told Grace that next month they would be going down to Thurley, her late husband's property in Hertfordshire, so as to avoid the noisome air of London during the worst part of the plague season.

"Oh, must we go away, madam? I'm sure it will be a great benefit, only I am not accustomed to the country."

"And you don't want to go there, sweetheart?"

Mrs. Tabor was not at all surprised. Town-bred herself, she dreaded these annual trips to Hertfordshire, to that large, unfriendly house surrounded by empty spaces. The rough lanes always seemed to be inches deep in mud, not that it mattered for they led nowhere in particular, while as for the inhabitants, both gentry and villagers looked down their noses at the rich newcomers from the City. As long as her husband was alive Mrs. Tabor had been forced to endure this yearly exile. Now he was dead she might have escaped, but having Grace to care for, she felt it was her duty to take the child out of reach of the plague.

Immediately after dinner Mrs. Tabor took a short rest, and Philadelphia sat down to her daily practice at the virginals. Grace knew how to seize her opportunity; murmuring something about helping Martha in the kitchen, she ran down the back stairs and then out into the street, confident that she could count on an hour of freedom before she was missed. Crossing Cheapside at its widest stretch, she made her way between the booths of dairy produce to the corner where two church spires leant towards each other above a cluster of small shops and she was caught in the interwoven shadows of St. Mary Magdalen, Milk Street, and All Hallows, Honey Lane.

She tiptoed into St. Mary's and bobbed down in a pew near the back for a few seconds of inarticulate prayer. Then she settled herself to contemplate the monumental tomb that was being constructed on the north wall of the church. It was a memorial to a wealthy merchant who had died recently, and when it was finished the effigies of the dead man and his wife would be seen kneeling devoutly under a canopy of wrought stone, while their fourteen children were shown in relief all round the base of the tomb. The big alabaster effigies had been brought to the church already complete, and were propped against the wall, swaddled in sacking, but the raised figures of the children had to be done on the spot. Eight sons in single file faced their six sisters along the side of their parents' grave. The boys were remarkably alike, except that they were graduated in size from the eldest at the front to the two little ones at the end of the line, each carrying a skull as a sign that he had died before the parents. The girls, too, were so many peas in a pod, but the sculptor had put in a few individual touches; one of the sons was reading a prayer-book, another had his hand on his heart, while several daughters were weeping and one was mopping her eyes with a handkerchief so real that it

166

looked more like linen than stone.

There was a very large man lying prostrate on his stomach in the aisle, patiently chipping out a decorative border at the foot of the tomb. Grace knew him well by sight, though in fact she could see nothing of him at this moment except his enormous backside and the patched soles of his boots. He was Melchior Breda, an immigrant stone-carver from the Low Countries and the employer of her dear friend Coney.

At first she thought he was alone; she could see no sign of Coney. Then she heard a slight movement which made her look up, and she was able to catch a glimpse of him standing on the raised tomb and almost hidden by one of the black marble pillars of the canopy. He too was working on the monument, carrying out his master's design with minute stroke of the chisel, so that inch by inch between them they covered every surface and made the bare stone flower.

Grace had started to come and sit in the church very soon after the disastrous morning when she and Mrs. Tabor had met Coney in the street outside. At first

167

he would not speak to her; he used to go stalking by with his head turned away, pretending not to know she was there. Until one day she was crying, and he came and sat beside her, gripping her hand and not saying anything, so that they made up their differences without any troublesome arguments, and since then they had been meeting in the church two or three times a week.

Melchior Breda seemed to accept her visits with placid approval. She was not sure if he understood her position; his English was extremely bad and his head was generally in the clouds, so he probably took it for granted that she was nothing more than a maidservant. In any case he must know that there was no harm in the quiet and sober talks they were able to have in church. Only once, when there was a wedding at St. Mary's, the stone-carvers weren't able to go in, and Coney had taken Grace for a walk. They had strolled along Aldersgate Street, passed St. Bartholomew's Hospital, till they came to London Wall. Feeling very venturesome, they had gone out of the City into Moorfields, a desolate, marshy place that had recently been drained and still had a strange, drowned landscape which looked as though it wasn't yet accustomed to the sun. It was the favourite haunt of courting couples, philosophers and lunatics, and also of the laundresses who went out there to do the City's washing and dried it on the grass. They did not meet any philosophers or lunatics, but presently Coney put his arms round Grace and kissed her on the mouth. And all of a sudden she knew that this what she had been waiting for. She knew why she had felt so uncomfortable being cajoled and caressed by Joel Downes; not because kissing was wrong in itself (which was the gloomy nonsense that had been thrashed into her by Mr. Tucker) but because it would always be wrong for her to kiss anyone except Coney. They had loved each other since they were small children, far more than most children would, for each had been the other's whole family.

She was thinking about all this as she waited in the cool austerity of the high-vaulted church. At last Melchior Breda clambered to his feet, a huge man with a jolly, red face.

"You may haf one short rest, boy," he said to Coney in his outlandish accent. "The young maiden here is come."

Coney jumped down from the tomb, somehow managing to arrest his jump in mid-air, when he remembered where he was, so that he landed with some pretence of reverence, and came across to join her in the pew.

"Well met, sweeting. I didn't think you'd come today."

"I had to see you, to tell you — Coney, she's taking me away!"

"Where to?" he demanded.

After she had explained, he laughed at her evident despair. "A few weeks' holiday in the country — there's nothing very terrible in that, surely? And the time will soon pass."

"I hope you won't have finished the monument and gone off somewhere else before I get back."

"Not much fear of that. And even if we had, I dare say we shall be going to one of the other churches around here, for so many people have been in to admire my master's work, and he has the offer of plenty more commissions. And because he has so much work, he is letting me watch all he does, and copy the easy bits whenever I can. It's the only way to learn, and I'm lucky to have the chance. When I'm a few years older, Mr. Breda says I shall be able to set up on my own and earn a good living too, for there's no shortage of work if you have the skill to do it."

"Won't it matter that you never served an apprenticeship?"

Grace had heard so much about apprentices since going to live with the Tabors. All their friends were continually making plans for their children and discussing the necessity of binding a small boy to the right master. As for any boy who was not properly apprenticed, as far as the City Companies were concerned he didn't exit. It wasn't a division between wealth and poverty. Although the Goldsmiths and Mercers were nearly all rich men, there were lesser Companies, like the Cobblers, or the Upholsterers, who sold second-hand goods and conducted funerals — their members were often poor, yet they could pass on to their sons the privilege of belonging to a craft. For children born outside the charmed circle, it was hard to get in, especially if they were foundlings like Coney who had never known their fathers. Not for them to hear the promise that the bells pealed out over the City: 'Turn again, Whittington, thrice Lord Mayor of London.'

Having learnt these things, she had begun to feel anxious about what would happen to Coney.

He had no fears on the subject as he tried to explain.

"It doesn't signify much for a stone-carver whether or not he's gone through all those legal forms. It's not as though I wanted to be a mason . . . "

"But I thought that's just what you did want! Carvers and masons — what's the difference?"

"Masons build houses. They have several fraternal crafts, bricklayers, tilers, and so forth, and some of them are also carvers. But there are plenty of carvers who don't choose to do anything else. That's what I want to be, an alabaster-man, working in churches or furnishing heraldic screens and chimney-pieces in great men's houses. There aren't enough alabasterers to go round, so no one troubles to ask where they come from. They'll accept strangers from the North of England or foreigners from the Netherlands, so why not a bastard from the Charity Hospital?"

Grace looked admiringly at Coney. His blue eyes were brilliant with enthusiasm, and his thatch of fair hair was standing on end; she longed to comb it into place. His shoulders had broadened in the last few months. His hands were strong and gentle. She was filled with loving confidence.

"I'll need a patron," he was saying, "when the time comes. And as soon as I have a little money saved, we'll be married. If you can wait for me so long."

"You know I will."

"They'll try to pair you off with some fat merchant or other, you see if they don't. Are you certain you can refuse?"

"Yes, because Mrs. Tabor is so kind, she would never force me to marry against my will. And indeed I think she may have trouble finding a bridegroom for me. Her rich friends look askance at me, they aren't certain whether to believe . . . "

She broke off. Coney disapproved strongly of the way she was imposing on Mrs. Tabor, and she did not want to draw his attention to it.

"I'd leave there tomorrow," she said with a slight gulp, "only I've nowhere to go. And — and I dare not confess, for fear of what they might do to me."

"No need to go looking for trouble. You'll have to stay there and keep your mouth shut until I'm able to take you away. And I tell you what, Grace: you shouldn't condemn yourself to sackcloth and ashes. So long as you don't let her settle a fortune on you, or make a great marriage under false pretences, I can't see that you're doing much harm. After all, you earn your keep, don't you? What with sewing and cooking and listening to the old woman's stories, I reckon you're worth as much as that fine gentlewoman she has dancing attendance on her."

As she dawdled her way back along

174

Milk Street, blinking at the sunlight, Grace considered what Coney had said. Although she was no longer so frightened of being unmasked, her conscience was a great deal more sensitive than it had been; she was now able to see shaded degrees of right and wrong that she had never perceived before. It was true, as Coney said, that she could stay in Goldsmiths' Row without robbing Mrs. Tabor of a vast sum of money. But suppose she remained there several years and then ran away with Coney (and she did not think she would be allowed to marry him, so they would have to run away). Wouldn't that be a wicked thing to do to her benefactress? Mrs. Tabor's daughter had run away with her lover and never come home. How would the old woman feel if the girl she accepted as her grandchild played the same trick?

Grace paused at the corner of Cheapside, waiting for a break in the traffic. Some horsemen passed in front of her, a cart loaded with vegetables, and then a curious sight: two sturdy fellows dragging a hurdle on which a dejected elderly man was seated, with his hands strapped behind him. Dangling from a cord round his neck there was a stale loaf of bread, and this made the whole situation plain. He was a baker who had been caught selling short weight.

She was very sorry for the man as he crouched on his hurdle, bumping over the cobbles and trying to avoid catching anyone's eye. How dreadful it must be to know that his customers and neighbours were seeing him publicly disgraced. Even so, there were worse fates.

She and Philadelphia had been walking past the pillory one day last week. There was a man pinioned in the usual backbreaking position, with his head and hands stuck through the sockets. This was a familiar sight, yet it had drawn quite a crowd, and the prisoner was whimpering and moaning in a very disturbing manner. When she saw the reason, Grace had felt sick with horror. For some specially grave crime the wretched man had been pinned to the pillory with a nail through each ear.

She had not managed to find out what he had done, or whether women were liable to such punishment. Was it (for instance) the sort of sentence you might receive for impersonating a lost heiress in order to inherit a fortune?

She could not possibly risk a confession.

15

"YOU add a little water," said Laurence. "And then stir it into a thick paste. So."

The powdered enamel, which was bright green, had been ground in the pestle and mortar. On the workbench lay the pendant that he was about to decorate. It was an intricate design and when it was finished would display a white and gold unicorn, about an inch high, against a thicket of green leaves and crystal berries. At the moment the pendant had a bare and skeletal appearance; the rock-crystal would be inserted at the end, and so would the unicorn's body, which was to be made of one large baroque pearl. The leaves were outlined in gold and each one hammered into a shallow cavity to receive the coloured enamel.

Laurence began to charge the dented surfaces with minute blobs of green paste. It was extraordinary that the hands of a grown man could manoeuvre with such wonderful dexterity on so small a scale; he never spilt a drop or smudged a line.

The two apprentices watched him, spellbound. Will was biting his tongue in suspense, Sam asking endless questions, which Laurence always took the trouble to answer.

The green leaves were all filled in; Laurence laid the pendant carefully in an iron dish and put it by the fire to dry out. When it had stopped steaming, he placed it in a cradle directly over the open furnace so that the paste should heat and liquefy. Once it was allowed to cool, the substance would harden to that gleaming patina which gave champlevé enamel its luxurious brilliance.

Joel stood watching the trio by the fire. His feelings towards his new master had subtly altered since that battle over the anvil. It was odd, he ought to have disliked Laurence even more. But then his dislike of Laurence had not been based on ordinary jealousy, and he was too single-minded a craftsman to be jealous of anyone whose work he honestly admired; there was no virtue in this, you simply could not reject beauty or the hand that made it.

Though he'd rejected Laurence's pictures, without really looking at them, which was a pity, for if he had looked properly he would almost certainly have guessed that of course it was Laurence himself who had designed and made the case for the portrait of Walter Brand which he had brought with him from the Continent. Brand had let him submit the miniature and its case to the Goldsmiths' Company as his masterpiece; Joel had discovered this eventually and it made him feel very small.

There was an open box of baroque pearls on the bench, he picked out a couple of them at random, playing with them in his hand. Unusually large, they were always badly misshapen, not fit to use in necklaces like ordinary pearls — the word baroque meant rough and lumpy in Moorish or some such foreign tongue — but the creamy-textured monsters were now much in demand for ornamental jewellery, the strange contours suggesting possible themes. What could you make of this one? A cornucopia, a swan, a sleeping cupid? He felt he would like to try out a few conceits of his own. Laurence's exquisitely tiny and sparkling fantasies had opened up whole new worlds that he wanted to explore. If he could pluck up courage to ask Laurence's permission.

"Don't forget to put them back," said a cool voice behind him.

"What?" he asked stupidly.

"Those two baroque pearls," said Laurence.

Joel dropped them into the box, flushing with mortification. "If you think I meant to steal them . . . "

"My dear Joel! Have I ever accused you of stealing? It's true you are inclined to regard my family's property as yours by right, but that's my fault, or my uncle's fault — whoever's to blame, we know it isn't you."

Joel turned and walked over to the other side of the workshop, picked up a silver porringer and began to polish it with such vigour that he made a large dent in one side. There was no hope of conciliating Laurence, he was sure of that now. Laurence mistrusted him too deeply, which was ironic, for he hadn't a scrap of evidence to back up his doubts about Grace. Joel thought that his suspicion and his dislike both stemmed from the same cause; Laurence could not forgive his former hostility, or the many scornful and indiscreet remarks that must undoubtedly have been repeated to him.

In which case, the future was bleak; Laurence might decide to turn him off without ceremony, he was practically penniless, he still hadn't received the whole of the promised reward for finding Grace, and as for his hope of marrying her, he could say good-bye to that if he stopped working for the Tabors. Unless he went ahead with his courtship straight away? Mrs. Tabor might not yet be ready to welcome him as a suitor, but he thought he could see his way around that difficult.

He found an opportunity to try his luck that very evening, for Philadelphia had gone to visit some friends of her family who lived in Blackfriars, so it was easier to manage a private meeting with Grace. After supper, instead of going off to his lodging, he hung around until he saw her go upstairs to her bedchamber. He followed her cautiously, gave a light rap on the door, and went in, without waiting for an answer.

Grace was standing by the dressing-chest in a ring of candle-light staring at her reflection in a small steel mirror. She turned, startled.

"Joel! You can't come in here! What do you want?"

"To talk with you."

The big blue eyes grew apprehensive. "Is — is anything wrong? Have they found out?"

"No, how could they?"

"Then why . . . "

"Come over here and I'll tell you."

He perched himself on the edge of the bed she shared with Philadelphia, and coaxed her to sit beside him, while he began to tell her how pretty she was, how seldom he was able to see her alone, how anxious he was to know whether she liked him as much as he liked her.

Grace stood up. "Will you please leave me now, Joel. You know you ought not to have come."

She spoke with a dignity she could not

have achieved a few months ago. She had learnt something in Goldsmiths' Row.

Joel got up too. It was no use talking, he'd have to take action. He pulled her into his arms and began to fondle her. There was an impression of soft, warm skin, the scent of rosewater, a drift of hair like stranded silk — and then she turned on him like an infuriated kitten and slapped his face.

He would never have believed it of her.

"You little shrew!" he complained, between annoyance and amusement, rubbing his cheek.

Where had this new spirit come from? Surely she hadn't got herself a lover already? he could not think of any likely candidate; it was true that he had once seen her alone in the street, which had surprised him, but she was only going into a church. Of course she had been brought up uncommonly pious; perhaps that was still a stumbling-block.

"Don't misunderstand me," he said. "I'm not asking you to do anything wrong. There's no sin in wanting to get married, is there?"

"Married? You and me?" She looked thunderstruck.

"Why not?" He smiled. "I think I must have chosen you for my wife the very first instant I saw you in Southwark, caring for that swarm of children. I suppose that's why I took such pains to rescue you from that place."

Grace did not answer at once. Then she said, inconsequently, "Mrs. Tabor would not favour your suit."

He knew that already, but he thought that if Grace wanted the match, she would be able to twist the old woman round her finger. This was his new plan. He must persuade Grace that he was the right husband for her, if possible with love and kindness — he was sure he could accomplish that in the end, only he hadn't got unlimited time. He had another weapon in his hand, and if she was recalcitrant he would have to use that. It was a fair means to an end, considering who and what she was.

"I'm sure Mrs. Tabor would listen to you," he said still hoping that gentler methods would prevail, "if you told her that you would like to marry me."

185

"But I shouldn't like it at all," retorted Grace with unflattering promptness. "I don't wish to marry you and what's more, I won't do it"!

Joel felt his temper rising. Perhaps he had started out too complacently, regarding Grace as a lay-figure in his plans, but since he had kissed her mouth, and run his fingers through her moonlight-coloured hair — yes, and since he had met the challenge of unexpected resistance — he had discovered some urgent new reasons for marrying her. And here she was, saying she didn't fancy him, the impudent bitch. After all he had done for her; it was intolerable.

"Am I not good enough for you now?" he enquired. "The heiress is holding out for a greater prize? Think again, my dear. No other man, however wealthy, can give you as much as I have given you already — all the benefits of Goldsmiths' Row, poured into the lap of a nameless pauper. Is it so strange that I should wish to share them with you?"

"I — I would rather give up the benefits."

"Oh, would you?" he said, stung by this insult. "Very well, then: we'll put your self-denial to the test. Either you agree to a marriage between us, or I tell Laurence that you are an imposter."

She gave a gasp of fright, and backed away from him, not trying to hide her aversion. "You daren't tell Laurence. He'll guess we were in league together, and you'll be punished too."

"No, for I shall tell him that I was completely deceived in you and that I've only just found you out. I shall play the part of injured innocence, and they'll believe every word I say."

This was empty bluster, and he knew it. But Grace's fears of discovery had always been exaggerated, and she was not a very logical thinker. She was now terrified, but even so she made no effort to save herself by giving him the answer he wanted.

This made him furious.

"On your own head be it," he told her angrily. "You may yet find there are worse fates than being married to me. Good grief, when I think how scared you've always been of that fellow Tucker!

What do you think they'll do to you in the Bridewell?"

This time he scored a complete victory.

Grace stumbled towards the bed and subsided there, shivering. She looked white and sick, but no longer seemed able to make any protest. She just stared up at him in dull desperation.

He knew that she would do anything he asked her now. And then discovered, to his consternation, that it was no use — he simply could not go on coercing this pitifully defenceless child, not for half a dozen fortunes. Such ambitious schemes seemed perfectly practical, any holiday afternoon, on the apron stage at the Rose Theatre, where corruption, rape and violence flourished in a world of unalloyed ferocity. Real life was different.

He was disgusted to find he was too thin-blooded to emulate all those Roderigos and Gonzagos whose sinister philosophy he had taught himself to admire. Grace had begun to cry in a dreary way which made him feel both ashamed and exasperated.

After a brief hesitation he left her, crept downstairs and out into Cheapside. The street was nearly deserted and pleasantly cool at the end of the long day. He heard the familiar reassurance of the watch, coming from the direction of Lombard Street.

"Half-past nine of the clock and a fine summer's evening, and all's well."

Joel went back to his lodging in Bachelors' Alley, lay awake on his narrow bachelor's bed and gazed at the yellow blur of a lamplit window across the way, considering how he had got himself to such a pass. All was very far from well.

16

IT was dinner-time; Mrs. Tabor presided at one end of the oak table, behind a massive pigeon pie, while Laurence, in a cloud of steam at the other end, was carving his way through a joint of boiled salt beef. On one bench sat Mr. Zachary Downes, Ralph and Grace; on the opposite side, Edmund, Joel and Philadelphia. The two apprentices had their dinner with the manservant and maidservants at a lesser table where conversation was not allowed, though they got exactly the same food as their betters — one of Laurence's extravagant innovations; his uncle had never considered it necessary

Mrs. Tabor liked to look around her household of dutiful, hungry people, enjoying the reward of a hard morning's work. She also liked to dwell on the number of fashionable people she saw coming into the shop nowadays. Laurence was a kind and considerate nephew (apart from his refusal to recognise dear Grace as a member of the family, and he had let that matter slide into the background lately). She was proud of his success.

"I hope the Astons are taking note of your customers," she remarked. "the Martins too, and all our other neighbours. There was a coach this morning — I'nm sure it was grand enough for a lord."

"A knight's widow merely," said Laurence. "Which is not to be sneezed at. She bought those ear-rings you admired, Aunt — the fire-opal clusters with fancy-cut amethyst drops."

Mrs. Tabor considered this. Glancing down the table, her doting eye found its target.

"Grace must have some ear-rings," she announced. "You'd like that, wouldn't you, my dear? Pearls and crystals would become you, I think. We must get your ears pierced . . . "

"No, madam! Oh! Please don't make me!" cried Grace with a gasp of horror. She had dropped her knife, which fell on the floor, and sat pressing her hands over the lobes of her ears as though to protect them. They all looked at her in astonishment.

"It doesn't hurt," Mrs. Tabor told her. "Just a prick with a hot needle . . . "

Grace burst into tears.

"My dear child, no one is going to make you have your ears pierced against your will," said Zachary Downes. "But it is not such a fearful operation, I assure you."

Grace muttered something about being stood in the pillory.

"What on earth do you mean?" asked Philadelphia.

"I suppose she's thinking of that man that was pilloried a while back," volunteered Sam, who had nearly dislocated his neck at the other table, trying to follow what was going on. "That was a rare show! They had this fellow's ears pegged out against the head-board of the pillory, like skins drying in a tanner's yard, and he was bawling an squawking, and the blood spouting all over the place . . . "

Mrs. Tabor gave a bleat of protest, Grace gulped as though she was going to be sick, and Mr. Zachary told Sam to shut his mouth and get on with his dinner.

Sam grinned. "Can't do both at the same time," he murmured impenitently.

"Stop clowning, Sam," said Laurence in his deceptively casual voice.

"Yes, sir," said Sam, subsiding instantly. The boys now knew exactly how far they could go with Laurence, and exactly what would happen if they went too far. Which simplified matters for everyone.

Gradually Grace became more composed, Mrs. Tabor having kindly promised her that she need never do anything she didn't like. As soon as the meal was over, she escaped and hurried out of the room.

"Grace, what are you afraid of? No one's going to hurt you," said Joel, who was standing by the door. He put out his hand to try and stop her. His voice was unusually gentle, he looked anxious and concerned, but she pushed past him and rushed upstairs, with Mrs. Tabor clucking after her.

Laurence detained Philadelphia in the parlour. "What do you make of that?"

"I agree with Sam. The sight of that

poor wretch in the pillory has been preying on her mind, and no wonder. I used to have nightmares over some of the things I saw when I first came to London."

"Grace grew up in London. Among people who consider themselves able to predict the torments of eternal damnation — you'd think the punishments of this world would seem tame by comparison."

"I suppose you think pauper children ought to have thicker skins than the rest of us?"

"You know I didn't mean that. But I don't believe Grace's display just now was due to ignorance of the harsh world, or a tender heart. That girl's got a guilty conscience."

"How much longer are you going to go on insisting that she's an imposter?"

"I hope very soon to prove it."

"I dare say!" she flashed at him contemptuously. "I'm sure you'll stop at nothing to rid yourself of a rival who stands between you and a great deal of money."

"You were bound to interpret all my actions in terms of money," he said in that agreeable manner which he kept for his most biting remarks. "Filthy lucre! That's the only god a tradesman worships, isn't it? Even if it entails buying false witnesses and perjured evidence — I suppose those are the usual weapons of a man who stops at nothing?"

"I never meant to suggest anything so — so dastardly!" she stammered. "And I know you do care for other things. I can believe that you wish to protect your aunt . . . "

"Gracious of you!" he brushed aside her protests. "Let me remind you of a few facts, Mrs. Whitethorn. Six years ago I cared so little for money that I threw up my inheritance rather than sacrifice such talent as I possess to the tyranny of an old man who was living in the past. I never thought he'd put me back into his will; I never tried to persuade him. Yet when I came home to claim what was lawfully mine, nearly everyone in this house treated me as though I was a leper. Because I succeeded to my uncle's estate, I must therefore be scheming to get hold of my aunt's as well. Why should I? Don't you know that I can earn as much as I please? I'm a craftsman, I was bred to work for my living, which seems to me an honourable occupation — if I may dare to use such a phrase. But I can hardly hope to convince *you*. We belong to different worlds. It's a mystery to me why you ever came to Cheapside; you can't have expected to find a husband."

Philadelphia was speechless, so astounded by this attack that she had no answer ready. He waited for a moment, as though to give her a chance of hitting back; then he turned and left her.

One of the maids, seeing the coast was clear, came back to pile up the dishes and plates, making a great clatter about it. Philadelphia ignored her, staring out of the window at the neat clumps of marigold in the small, shady garden. Her mind was going round like a weathercock.

A great deal of what Laurence had said made her feel very uncomfortable; she and Joel had certainly got off on the wrong foot with him. That extraordinary composure made him seem selfishly indifferent to the rights of others, and the impression had been strengthened, right from the start, by the way he had flatly refused to consider Grace's claims on his family, even before he had heard the evidence. Perhaps she had misjudged him, just as he had been wrong about her, thinking her too proud for the people she was living with, too much of a fine lady. What could she have done to give him such an idea?

But these riddles were of minor importance. The sting of the whole encounter was in his parting shot, the cruel way he had jeered at her not having a husband. She had spent a year in Goldsmiths' Row without getting a single offer. She was a failure and everyone knew it, an old maid of twenty-two with a hideous blemish; nobody would ever want to marry her. Furious with herself, she blinked back the tears of self-pity.

She was too preoccupied to wonder what exactly was troubling Grace, though she got a hint of this a couple of days later, in the form of a question.

"Is it just you and me and my grandmother that are going to Thurley? No one else?"

"No one else to start with. There are servants at Thurley already, you know, and the maids here have to stay and keep this house running, for the shop will be open all the time we are away. I dare say Mr. Laurence will come down to Thurley; the property belongs to him now. And I believe your grandmother has invited her sister to pay her a visit, and all the Beck daughters and their children. At least we shan't want for company."

"I wondered — will Joel be there?"

"I doubt it."

Was the wind in that quarter? It would be very natural.

"Did you want him to come?" she asked.

"Oh, no! I'm glad he won't — I hate him!"

Philadelphia had to revise her opinion.

"Has he been pestering you?" she enquired. "If so, you must tell me; I don't mind tackling Master Joel, or better still, I'll inform his father . . . "

"You mustn't do that, you mustn't tell anyone! Del, promise me you won't."

Grace overwhelmed her with urgent and confusing entreaties, protesting that

Joel had never attempted any lovemaking, and unreasonably frightened of what he would do to her if he was accused of such a thing. It was useless to tell her that there was nothing he could do. Grace didn't listen, but just kept on twisting her hands and whispering that she wished people wouldn't meddle.

Philadelphia felt obliged to accept what she said and leave her in peace, but she could not help jumping to one unavoidable conclusion. Joel must have some hold over Grace. As to what sort of a hold it was, the most likely explanation was all too plain. If Grace was a conscious and deliberate impostor, the one person who certainly knew it was Joel.

This was a most disconcerting train of thought. Months ago Philadelphia had become convinced that Grace was the real Frances Tabor, and she wanted to go on believing it. She thrust the alternative out of her mind; she could not waste time pandering to such fancies at present, she was getting ready for the move to the country; it was of course necessary for them to take down all the usual items of bed-curtains, linen and plate. She worked hard, packing the stuff into hampers, helped by a revived Grace, who had cheered up as soon as she heard Joel wasn't coming to Thurley.

"I've never been to Hertfordshire," she chatted, one afternoon when they were rolling up a large set of couch-work hangings. "Is it near to Portsmouth, Del?"

"No, the other side of London. Why?"

"I had a friend called Nan Briggs who went to live in Portsmouth. She was my first friend at the Hospital; we were both of an age, though she came there the year after me. Her father was a sailor, and when her mother died Nan was put in the Hospital. She was there seven years, until she had passed her ninth birthday, and then her father married a widow in Portsmouth and fetched her away to live with them; I remember how we all envied her. We never saw her afterwards. I wonder what's become of her now. Why, she might be married."

Philadelphia said nothing. She was grappling with an uncompromising piece of arithmetic. Grace and this Nan were the same age. Nan was admitted to the Charity Hospital when she was two years old. *And Grace was already there.* Therefore she could not be Frances Tabor, who had arrived in Southwark with her foster-parents three years later. What was more, she could not be the supposedly innocent foundling whose early memories of life outside the Charity Hospital had led her to believe that she might be the missing Frances. A child who was already in the Hospital at the age of two could not possibly have any memories of life before she got there.

Philadelphia squatted back on her heels and stared across the roll of curtains at Grace, who was kneeling behind them, meticulously pinning the folds, oblivious of what she had said. She looked so pretty and so good, such a credit to all they had done for her in Goldsmiths' Row. It now appeared that she was a wicked little liar. Yet she was so young, and it must have been a great temptation . . .

If I give her away, reflected Philadelphia, I suppose they'll hand her over to that brute in Southwark. Poor girl, how wretched he'll make her, it doesn't bear thinking of. Mrs. Tabor will be wretched, knowing she was deceived. No doubt Joel will be wretched also, which I dare say he deserves, but I have nothing against Joel and I think his family have been abominably treated by the Tabors. The one person who won't share in all this wretchedness is Laurence. He'll be cock-a-hoop. She admitted, guiltily, that this was the most disappointing aspect of the whole business.

She decided that she was not going to rush into a flood of accusations. She was going to think out the consequences slowly and impartially in the quiet of the country, and if Grace's pretensions had to be overthrown, a few more weeks' delay would make no difference. She had all sorts of high-minded reasons for thinking this. She was also extremely reluctant to have to go and tell Laurence that he was right and she was wrong.

17

PHILADELPHIA had stayed at Thurley the summer before, when John Tabor was alive, and soon after she had taken her place in his household. So she was not surprised by the size of the red brick mansion, the endless procession of lofty rooms that never got properly warm, the neglected garden or the tall grass that came right into the forecourt like an incoming tide. The great house at Thurley had been built the same year as Hampton Court, an imitation on a small scale, by a successful courtier who thought he was founding a dynasty. But his line had petered out in two generations, and the property was sold to Henry Angell, a Cheapside goldsmith, whose daughter, Bess Angell, had been the devoted friend of young Frances Tabor. Angell had a passion for buying houses, he bought them all over the place; the one at Enfield where Frances died was another. In the end his extravagance ruined him, the family retreated from Goldsmiths' Row, and Thurley was sold to John Tabor.

It was not clear whether he had bought it to help his old friend out of a hole, or because it was going cheap. He took very little interest in his noble estate, beyond sending his wife down there for a few weeks every summer; she was too browbeaten to refuse.

"It's not a friendly house, is it?" whispered Grace, daunted by her surroundings. "And I'm frightened of the servants."

Philadelphia thought that the servants were at the root of it; they were certainly very different from Mrs. Tabor's jolly, quick-spoken London maids who had been with her half a lifetime and were perfectly contented with their lot. It was a measure of their content that they had never resented the little foundling; the idea that she was Frances's long-lost baby appealed to their love of drama. They welcomed her in the kitchen and let her make herself useful. The servants at Thurley were very different: a sullen collection, intermarried and inbred, who lived soft all the year round inside the sheltering walls of the great house, and felt put upon during the few weeks that the family were in residence.

She decided that it was necessary to tackle the ringleader, whose name was Simeon Wacey, and who called himself the steward, though she suspected that he'd never been more than a butler, and not a very good one.

The servants must get up earlier, she told him; the chamber-maids must finish cleaning all the upstairs rooms by ten o'clock, and dinner must be on the table punctually at eleven.

"And while we are on the subject of food . . . "

"Peace, woman," intoned Wacey, making a gesture of dismissal with his fat, white hand. "It is not your duty to admonish me, and I do not choose to hear you."

"You are mistaken," said Philadelphia, who did not relish this form of address. "Mrs. Tabor has asked me to give you her orders."

"It is not customary for the mistress of the house to send messages to the steward through an inferior . . . " In his neat black, with his white collar, Wacey looked like an odiously condescending archdeacon. "I dare say such things are not understood where you come from. In my late master's time . . . "

"Your late master," Philadelphia informed him, "was the grandson of a dishonest Customs clerk, and all the world knows it. His forbears were counting on their fingers when mine were riding across Gloucestershire at the head of a troop of horse. And when there was a Tabor keeping his state as Lord Mayor of London. So don't try to stun me with your examples of gentility."

This put him out of countenance, and during the next week she bullied and persuaded him into getting the house shipshape and seeing that the servants did what they were told.

Wacey did his best to maintain his own importance, and finally came out with the time-honoured threat: all the servants were preparing to leave in a body. He added, as an afterthought, that no one in the village would dare to replace them.

Philadelphia had expected this, sooner or later. She had her answers ready. "We'll get servants from the City," she said airily.

He gave her a pitying smirk. "You won't get them to stay long in the country."

"But they may not be required to stay."

He stared at her. "What do you mean?"

"You can't surely suppose that a young man like Mr. Laurence Tabor will care to live in an ill-appointed house where he is ashamed to entertain his friends? I believe he is already in two minds about leaving Thurley," said Philadelphia, happily romancing as she went along. "He could afford to let the house stand empty for a year or two, while he waited for a suitable offer."

There was a baffled silence, while the steward worked out what could happen if he drove these interlopers too far. He then remembered that there was some urgent business needing his attention in the buttery, and withdrew, more in sorrow than in anger, leaving Philadelphia in symbolic possession of the great hall and feeling rather pleased with herself.

"Magnificent!" said an amused voice behind her. "We shan't have any trouble from him."

She was taken completely by surprise. Laurence was supposed to be miles away in Cheapside. Instead, he was standing just inside the oak screen that separated the hall from the front door, with the dust of travel on his boots and a distinctly ironic glint in his eye.

"I thought you were in London," she said stupidly.

"I wanted to make certain that everything was going well down here. I see I need not have troubled. Do you play chess, Mrs. Whitethorn? You were at least three moves ahead of that old villain."

"I don't know how much you overheard," she said, aware that she had been slightly carried away. "You must have thought it a great impertinence, my suggesting that you were going to shut the house."

"On the contrary. I thought it was a master-stroke." He put down his gloves and riding-whip, and stood looking out of the tall window at the glowing colours of a hot summer evening. "Could we go on talking out of doors? I must play my respects to my aunt, but I don't suppose she'll grudge me a stroll in the garden first."

Philadelphia was glad to get out into the warm, still air. The garden, so-called, was not much better than a wilderness, though you could still make out a ghost-pattern of throttled hedges and tufts of pinks and pansies visible under the weeds. The paths were freckled with moss, and the pleached alley so weighed down with ivy tendrils, and clambering roses running back to briar, it seemed as though the tunnel of living branches might collapse at any moment.

Laurence was still talking about Wavey. "I don't like the fellow, but I don't want to be too speedy in making changes that might not suit my aunt."

"Your aunt doesn't like him either. Nor does the Vicar."

"What's he done to annoy the Vicar? Too zealous in religion?"

"If you can call it that. He's for ever

trying to hunt out witches."

They had reached the edge of a small lake. The grass here was short, being steadily nibbled by a flock of geese. Their maid-in-waiting sat in the shadow of a hazel bush: a little, barefoot girl of about nine, who gazed at wonder at Laurence and Philadelphia but was too shy to return their greeting. The edge of the lake was thick with rushes, the surface of the water was a bright, opaque green, covered with a mesh of reeds that spread like the tentacles of a deep-sea monster.

Laurence sighed. "How I used to love this place. I learnt to swim in there; you wouldn't think it now."

"How old were you when your uncle came here?"

"Sixteen. But I was thinking of earlier days, when the Angell family had it. Bess Angell was my cousin Frank's dearest friend, and Bess's younger brother Tom was mine. I wish I could get news of them. I've entirely lost sight of them both . . . Tell me honestly, do you think I can set this garden to rights again, or has the ruin gone too far?"

"I'm sure it can still be done, though

it will cost you a mint of money before you're through." Which was a clumsy thing to have said; it was extraordinary how she could never talk to Laurence without getting on to the subject of money. "I mean," she explained carefully, "that I wouldn't encourage a poor man to saddle himself with so large an undertaking."

It was clear that he had been struck by the same uncomfortable association.

He said, hesitantly, "There's something I ought to say to you. I'm afraid that I was outrageously uncivil to you, just before you left Cheapside . . . "

"Don't say any more, sir," she interposed. "I think I was twice as uncivil to you, and I started first."

"All the same, I am sorry if I offended you . . . "

"Not the least in the world!" she assured him cheerfully.

This was a lie. He had as good as told her that she as too ugly to get a husband, and how could she escape from the pain of believing that was true? But as soon as she had recovered her temper, she had acquitted him of saying it on purpose. It was a thought in the back of his mind which had slipped out by accident, and it would not be fair to hold it against him. Better for her pride to pretend that she had not entirely taken in what he said.

"The next time you want me to hold my tongue," she suggested, "You'd better take a leaf from Wacey's book. Stand before me with your hand upraised, and say in a voice of great solemnity: 'Peace, woman!'"

"No, did he do that?" exclaimed Laurence, delighted. His eyes were full of laughter. "What an impudent rogue he is. And how I wish I'd been there!"

This put an end to any stiffness between them. They sauntered along by the water's edge and he began to discuss some of the improvements he wanted to make, asking her opinion.

This would be a good moment, thought Philadelphia, to tell him about Grace. That she's a cheat who's given herself away at last, and not his long-lost cousin. I don't think he would be unduly triumphant or vindictive. And he has the right to know.

He also had the right to a spell of ease and refreshment after his long ride from the City. And it seemed a pity to spoil such a pleasant evening. In the end she said nothing.

18

SOON the Beck family arrived in force at Thurley: Mrs. Beck, two of her married daughters with numerous children, and her younger daughter Judith. The Becks had not yet acquired a house in the country, and the redoubtable Hannah rather prided herself on this. They were honest merchant stock, perfectly content in their own state of life, not feeling it necessary to imitate the gentry — these protestations did not prevent her enjoying her sister's hospitality at Thurley and criticising everything she found there.

The married daughters were chiefly concerned with the health and safety of their children, who showed a tendency to eat too much ripe fruit and fall in the lake. Grace presented herself as an extra nursemaid. She was in her element, delighted to cosset and play with the babies and keep them out of mischief, and even Mrs. Beck had to admit that she was a patient, sensible girl who knew what she was about.

Philadelphia was expected to entertain Judith, which she found rather heavy going. Judith was very pretty and good, but she was dutiful to the point of dullness, and conversed only in prim, colourless monosyllables.

Laurence came down quite often from London. He began to get acquainted with his country neighbours, a thing his uncle and aunt had never managed to do. Occasionally he brought a friend with him for a short stay, and one of these was Mr. Walter Brand.

Philadelphia was a little surprised to meet Mr. Brand at Thurley, not because she would have considered him too proud to come, but in the present state of affairs she thought Laurence might have been too proud to ask him.

He seemed perfectly satisfied with the family party, and did not appear to be pining for any of the usual fashionable entertainments such as hunting, dancing, playing tennis and billiards, or performing masques.

The only fly in the ointment was Mrs.

Beck, as she dominated the dinner-table, patronising her sister, admonishing her grandchildren, and telling her daughters what to say and think.

She was particularly overbearing with Judith, whom she was carefully displaying as a possible bride for Laurence. You could not ask Judith to pass the salt without her mother chipping in, briskly scolding the poor girl for day dreaming, telling her to do as she was bid, explaining that Judith never took salt herself and why, with a eulogy about her excellent health since the age of five.

No wonder she's so silent, thought Philadelphia, when every word she utters provides more fuel for her mother's folly. She said as much to Walter Brand.

"It's monstrous!" he exclaimed. "Why does the girl allow herself to be turned into a doll, a puppet? Is she afraid of her mother? She's a grown woman, she ought to be able to speak with her own voice."

"I don't think she's afraid; I fancy her strict upbringing has simply given her a very strong sense of filial obedience. I dare say it won't do her any harm in the long run," added Philadelphia. "Most men prefer docility. She should make an excellent foil for a strong-minded husband."

"Provided he's strong-minded enough to bar the door against his mother-in-law!"

They were standing on the newly-mown grass outside the front door, just after dinner. Laurence was sitting on a stool, a little way off, making a charcoal sketch of an elm tree.

"Do you two want to ride," he asked. "I'll be with you directly."

"I'll go and change," said Philadelphia. "And I'll warn Judith to be ready also."

The four of them had fallen into the habit of riding together in the afternoons and singing madrigals in the evenings. They all had well-trained voices and enjoyed airing them in comparative peace; even Mrs. Beck knew better than to interrupt a group of singers in full spate. Mrs. Tabor sometimes hinted that Grace ought to make one of their little group, but Philadelphia paid no attention. She felt that Grace's ambiguous presence would upset the delicate balance of friendliness between herself and Laurence. And Grace certainly did not want to join them. She was younger than any of them, she could neither ride nor sing, she was frightened of Laurence and very much preferred being with the children. So Philadelphia was able to leave her behind with a clear conscience.

There was only one side-saddle at Thurley, so Philadelphia let Judith have it and herself put on breeches and rode cross-ways like a man, as she had done all her life. The fact that Mrs. Tabor and all the female Becks thought this behaviour unmaidenly caused her considerable amusement.

Presently the quartet were all assembled and mounted, Philadelphia on a handsome grey gelding who needed a lot of exercise and always set out from the stables with a swishing tail and a rolling eye.

The countryside was thickly wooded, and they rode from their own village of Thurley towards a hamlet called Little Pagwort, through tall groves of trees and along silent bridle-paths that lay deep in leaf mould. There were herds of deer moving around them, appearing and disappearing, shadow-dappled in the broken light of the sun pouring through the branches.

"You'll have to keep the numbers down," said Brand. "They're too thick on the ground. I take it your uncle had no use for the noble art of venery?"

"Not he. And I know very little of it as yet, but I mean to learn. You must give me some good advice."

"It seems a pity," said town-bred Judith, "to kill such graceful creatures."

Walter Brand and Philadelphia exchanged eloquent glances.

"If they were left to breed unchecked," said Brand, "the people of this island would soon starve."

"Why, is their meat so necessary to us?"

"It's not simply their meat, it's the damage they do. Look at that cornfield, all fenced around with stakes and hurdles; as it is, the deer break in whenever they can. If there were three times as many, and they were maddened by hunger, nothing would keep them out. They

219

would decimate the harvest. So some of them have to be killed, and if you lived in the country, you would soon come to enjoy the sport. I fancy Mrs. Whitethorn is a great huntress — are you not, madam?"

"I've never shot at driven deer, and I don't think I should care to. We hunt the Hart at force where I come from."

"What's that mean?" asked Judith.

"We chase our quarry across country with a pack of hounds, and follow them on horseback."

"And it may comfort you to know that the hunters are in nearly as much peril as their prey," said Laurence cheerfully. "They often break their necks."

They had ridden past the field of standing corn — this summer's crop for an entire community — and were now level with a second field that lay fallow and unfenced, ready to be ploughed for sowing the following season. The talk of hunting and the country sights had made Philadelphia restless. It wasn't enough to amble down the lanes at a sedate jog that suited Judith. She took her horse into the open field, and let him choose his own pace across the stubble.

She heard the drum of hoofbeats and the crackle of dry stalks behind her; glancing over her shoulder, she saw that Laurence was coming after her. She felt increasingly irritated by these Londoners and their town ways. Couldn't he leave her to ride by herself if she wished? Had she got to be continually hampered by an escort?

She touched the grey gelding's side with her heel, and he broke into a gallop.

At the far corner of the field she dropped into another lane, and turned to the right. They were going more slowly now, but still at a steady canter. It was a joy to be away from streets and houses and people and aimless chatter, moving freely through a solitary world of green grass and clear sky. She was just thinking this when her horse put his foot in a rabbit-hole, pecked and almost fell. She pitched out of the saddle and landed ignominiously on the ground.

For a moment she was so surprised that she just stayed there, swearing. She was not hurt, but furious at her own incompetence. The horse had recovered his footing and started back along the lane, the way they had come. She was horrified to see that he was going lame. Laurence had now appeared from the stubble field, and was coming towards them.

Philadelphia stood up, feeling extremely mortified. She had made a fool of herself, proved that she did require an escort, and lamed a valuable horse, unpardonably, through careless riding.

She watched Laurence reach for the grey's loose rein and coax him round. As he approached, with both horses under control, she had time to reflect that even if he hadn't been brought up to hunting and falconry, like a country gentleman, Laurence had travelled half across Europe on horseback, and he looked remarkably well in the saddle.

"You're not hurt?" he asked quickly. "What happened?"

"I let him stumble into a rabbit warren, and I've lamed him for you. I'm very sorry."

"Never mind that," he said, dismounting. "So long as you are not injured?"

"Oh, I'm as right as rain."

"And I don't think Grey Gallant is much the worse, either. He's worked a shoe loose, that's all." Laurence had inspected the damage; now he let go of the horse's hoof, patted his shoulder and straightened up. "If we continue along this way, we'll come to Great Pagwort where I believe they have a smithy. Will you let me put you up on my mare? I'll lead Gallant."

"That seems a poor sort of justice," said Philadelphia, "considering that Gallant's accident was entirely my doing."

"My dear Mrs. Whitethorn, do you think I should care to be seen riding about the countryside, while you trudged beside me on foot?"

"No, I suppose not."

"You suppose right," said Laurence, with a perfectly straight face and a voice full of mockery. As he lifted her on to the mare he had the virtuous expression of someone engaged in heaping coals of fire. Philadelphia tried to feel indignant, but found she wanted to laugh.

In fact he did not have to walk far. It was less than half a mile to the Great

223

Pagworth crossroads, where they found a cluster of cottages, a tavern, a horse pond and a blacksmith's shop. The smith was busy mending a broken spit, but would soon attend to Grey Gallant's shoe.

"You have a snug place here," said Laurence, looking around the forge.

The smith noted the way he eyed the row of massive tools that hung by the fire.

"Maybe your honour has a fancy to try your hand?"

Laurence said meekly that he would never make a blacksmith.

"Those are the true sons of Vulcan," he said to Philadelphia, as they sauntered away together, leaving both horses tethered outside the forge. "What I can do is puny by comparison."

"Come, Mr. Tabor! It is not like you to be so modest."

He laughed, taking her arm, as they rounded the edge of a small wood. They came on a fallen tree-trunk that was blocking the path. By common consent they sat down on it, to contemplate the view. There was a bracken-covered slope running down to a little stream, and on the other side a clump of oaks and more bracken, running over the opposite hillside like a turbulent sea.

"It's a fair prospect," she remarked.

"Yes."

She discovered that he was not admiring the Arcadian scene, he was looking at her legs as they stretched in front of her, slender and well-shaped, in russet-coloured breeches and boots of Spanish leather. After a moment she asked, "Did you never see a woman in breeches before?"

"Certainly," he retorted, "but never one more admirably designed."

He studied her with an air of speculation. The world around them had suddenly become very still. Philadelphia thought that he was going to kiss her. She was wearing a mask to protect her skin from the rays of the sun; almost unconsciously she untied the cord and slipped it off.

She had been kissed several times at harvest feasts and Christmas revels (Usually in the dark and by men who were too drunk to notice her disfigurement, as her sister-in-law always pointed out on the following day.)

Philadelphia had schooled herself not to expect anything more from these encounters than the immediate pleasure. That was what she expected now, with a desire so keen that it was almost painful. It was astonishing not to say disconcerting, that Laurence could make her feel like this.

But something had gone wrong. Instead of taking her in his arms, he just sat there, apparently trying to brace himself for an act he found intensely difficult. It was because of her scar, of course. He might have forgotten it while she was masked. Now it must be hideously repulsive. Perhaps he could not bear to touch her. She shut her eyes, as though by shutting him out she could herself become invisible.

"Don't do that," said the quiet voice beside her.

"What?"

"Deny me every pleasure I have a mind to. First I must not stare at your legs, and now you won't let me gaze into your eyes."

"Oh. I thought you had gazed long enough."

"I wasn't sure what I could see."

"I can tell you that," she said, rallying. "Your own portrait in miniature, twice reflected!"

This seemed to amuse him, and to gain a respite for them both, she asked whether he had ever painted a self-portrait.

"A dozen times at least. I'm my own favourite subject."

You would be, she thought, surveying the cameo features of that almost too perfect profile.

"I never distract myself by talking while I'm working," he explained. "Or grumble at having to hold the same pose too long. Or haggle with myself over the price."

"And what happens to these masterpieces when they are finished?"

"Oh, I give them to my valentines," he replied airily. "They are much in demand among the lovelorn maids of Cheapside — surely you might have guessed? Or did you think I'd hidden them at the back of a high shelf with poor old Zachary's mazer bowls that nobody wants to buy?"

As a rule Philadelphia enjoyed this sort of nonsense, but today she had lost her sense of proportion and Laurence's wit seemed hardly more than a transparent cloak for his intolerable vanity.

She was not going to encourage him any further; she was not one of his spaniel-women, begging for favours. She began to move away from him, just as he finally made up his mind and leant forward to draw her into his arms. She wriggled out of his grasp and there was a slight scuffle. Laurence tried to get a firmer grip and Philadelphia gave him a buffet in the chest, just as Judith and Walter rode into view round the corner of the wood.

Philadelphia had a confused vision over Laurence's shoulder, of the two horses, immensely tall from that angle, and the two disapproving and unsmiling faces above them.

Giving Laurence an angry push, she scrambled to her feet and started brushing the twigs off her jacket.

It was all made much more awkward by the solemnity of Judith and Brand. Even Laurence's assurance had failed him;

when they had reclaimed Grey Gallant and the mare, and were all four mounted once more, he paid no further attention to Philadelphia but rode ahead with Judith, who immediately began talking to him in a low, complaining voice.

Philadelphia was left with Brand.

"I hope you did not have much trouble finding us," she said. "I am afraid I have disrupted your ride."

"It's of no consequence," he replied shortly.

She was surprised by his ungracious manner. It was one thing for Judith, brought up by Mrs. Beck in a state of good shopkeepers' morality, to be offended by what she might have taken for an amorous romp. But Brand was a man of the world, she would not have expected him to care a straw. Why should he?

Unless he thought she was deliberately trying to ensnare his friend, and despised her for it. He must know that Laurence would never be content with an ugly wife.

They did not speak again on their ride back to Thurley.

19

"WOULD you like to hear a secret?" offered Mrs. Tabor.

"If you wish to tell me one, madam."

Philadelphia was tired; she had slept badly, wondering all night how she ought to have handled Laurence yesterday afternoon, and exactly how she appeared to him and his friends. A hungry virgin, desperate for love? Or a calculating one, determined to get married? She was tidying Mrs. Tabor's workbox, and went on winding the silks while she listened without much interest to what her mistress was saying.

Until her attention was suddenly caught.

" . . . My nephew Laurence and my niece Judith are secretly betrothed!"

Philadelphia laid down the last bobbin of silk and began to pick up the pins in the bottom of the box. She felt icy cold.

"It has always been a dear wish of mine that they should marry."

"It sounds an excellent match, madam." She had managed to find her voice. "But why should it be a secret?"

"Ah, that's the question! But I'll tell you what happened. I was here in my bedchamber an hour ago when I heard voices in the gallery. I didn't mean to listen, only there was someone crying. So I looked out and it was Judith; she was with Laurence, and he was trying to comfort her. He said — I remember the words exactly — he said: 'You must surely understand that no man wants his wife's mother ruling the roost.' And she said: 'It will be different when we are married.' Then they went away together down the stairs, so I heard no more. But you can see how it is, Del — my sister has been so overbearing that they prefer to keep their news a secret for the present. I only hope she won't put him off altogether. She will interfere in everyone's concerns; and one day I dare say she'll be sorry for it," said Mrs. Tabor with a pardonable touch of malice.

She went on discussing the betrothal, leaving Philadelphia free to think her own bitter thoughts. So that was the explanation of yesterday's comedy. There had been some sort of a lovers' quarrel, and Laurence had used her merely as a weapon to torment Judith. Which accounted for Judith's distress, and for Brand's disapproval; he was probably in Laurence's confidence. Everyone knew except me, thought Philadelphia angrily. I was left in ignorance to make a fool of myself.

Laurence and Brand were going back to London that day, and she was glad of it. There was dinner to be got through, but it was possible to sit there, eating little, saying less, and staring at her plate. Immediately afterwards she retired to her bedchamber with a not entirely imaginary headache.

She lay on her bed, telling herself there was no need to be overcome by such a trivial misadventure. She had hovered on the brink of dalliance with a man who was playing her off against another young woman; what was so terrible in that?

She knew the answer well enough.

Somehow in the last few weeks or even days she had allowed herself to become physically and mentally enthralled by Laurence Tabor. She was fascinated by his strength and by the graceful air of detachment that concealed it; by his good looks (even though she considered them excessive) and by the voice that mocked while it charmed. The hands which created so much delight: the exquisite miniature portraits, the fantasies of wrought gold, gleaming with pearls and dancing with colour and light. You would say that only a fine and sensitive mind could conceive work of such quality.

There were sounds in the courtyard below; Laurence and Brand with a couple of grooms, were preparing to start on their journey. She had an almost irresistible impulse to take a last look at him before he went away. She rolled over on the bed, biting her knuckles, refusing to give in to this shameful weakness. Presently she heard the little cavalcade set off down the avenue. She waited for several minutes, and then got up and glanced out of the window.

They had vanished out of sight. The

only person visible was Grace, strolling on the grass in idle unconcern: the stable cat was running along beside her, stalking field-mice. She flicked her fingers at him, and he sprang on to her shoulder and rubbed his soft black head against her cheek.

What a strange creature she is, thought Philadelphia. I wonder who her true parents were. I ought to have told Laurence that I caught her out in that lie. But she pushed this knowledge to the back of her memory. She had no wish to seek for any further encounters with Laurence.

One good thing happened at the end of that week: Mrs. Beck returned to the City for the lying-in of yet another daughter. She took Judith with her, but left her two eldest behind; Dorothy Philips and Joan Bradshaw with all their children. The peaceful, unexacting company of her nieces and their families suited Mrs. Tabor very well.

"I've never felt so comfortable in this house before," she said one rainy afternoon when the women were sitting in the long gallery. Some of the older boys and girls were at the far end, playing a noisy game without disturbing their elders; Grace was amusing the little ones by telling them rhymes.

"Grace does so dote on children," murmured Mrs. Tabor fondly.

"I hope she'll still be doting when she's borne as many as I have," said Dorothy Philips, who was enduring her seventh pregnancy.

Having recited Little Jack Horner and several other favourites, Grace began a jingle that Philadelphia had ever heard before;

"A golden house in a golden row,
Where the golden people come and
    go;
With crystal windows and pearly
    doors,
Silver ceilings and golden floors,
Golden tables and silver chairs,
Golden apples and silver pears,
And every night as you lie in bed,
A silver dream in a golden head."

This had an extraordinary effect. Mrs. Tabor and her two nieces all spun round to stare at the girl who knelt on the rush-strewn floor, rocking one of Dorothy's little boys to the rhythm of her voice.

"It's an age since I last heard that," said Joan Bradshaw.

"Yes," said her sister with a tremor of excitement, "but don't you see what it means?"

Mrs. Tabor had risen and was bearing down on Grace.

"I knew we should be given a sign, I knew the truth would prevail in the end! I always said you were my Frank's daughter, and now we can prove it!"

"Prove what?" asked Grace, looking more alarmed then delighted as she was clasped in a grandmotherly embrace. "Oh, please, what have I done?"

"That rhyme, sweetheart — it was made especially for your mother. Didn't Cicely Fox tell you so? Can't you remember?"

"No," said Grace slowly, "I've known it so long, I thought it was something everyone knew, like Jack Horner . . . Oh! Do you mean that the golden house was our house, in Goldsmiths' Row? I never thought of that."

"It is a little fanciful," said Mrs. Tabor seriously. "We don't have gold and silver furniture. Mr. William Tabor put that in to make your mother laugh. He was Laurence's father, and greatly attached to Frank; he had no daughter of his own. He made that rhyme for her when she had the measles and no one ever heard it outside our family — Doll and Joan can bear me out."

Her nieces both agreed.

"I remember how I envied Frank," said Dorothy, "living in a golden house and having an uncle like Mr. William Tabor. He was very handsome and witty — like Laurence. How it all comes back! I'd forgotten that rhyme for twenty years."

"I don't think we ever taught it to Edmund or Judith," said Joan.

"No, because they were the youngest of the family. They were very small when Frank ran away." Dorothy broke off hastily, but Mrs. Tabor had not noticed, she was occupied in making a fuss of Grace, who had gone white with emotion and seemed lost for words. The children all began to catch the enthusiasm, and there was a great deal of talking and laughing, Dorothy remarking to her sister that their mother would be very much put out. She sounded rather pleased.

Philadelphia joined in the rejoicings without saying very much.

"What's your opinion?" she asked Joan later. "Do you think that Grace's knowing this rhyme is enough to prove that she is your cousin's daughter?"

"Yes, I think she must be. I can see no other answer, for that verse was never known outside our families — and certainly not among the poor people over in Southwark, where Grace grew up. She can only have learnt it from Cicely Fox, who used to be her mother's nurse."

"I suppose it might be suggested that she first heard it after she arrived in Goldsmiths' Row."

"I don't think that's possible. We have none of us recited those lines for years, my children were never taught them until today. The fact is that after Frank ran off, and more still after she died, everything that concerned her was prohibited, not to be spoken of. So the rhyme was gradually forgotten. I couldn't have told you the words myself until Grace brought them back to me . . . But what's your purpose in asking this?" Joan glanced curiously at Philadelphia. "I thought you were one of Grace's chief champions?"

"I always have been," said Philadelphia, collecting herself. "My only fear is for your aunt. She has little understanding of evidence, and I don't wish her to set her heart on a definite proof and then be told that it still isn't good enough."

This satisfied Joan, and gave Philadelphia time to think. Having privately changed her view of Grace, she was now mystified. This latest episode was completely unexpected, and she did not know what to make of it. When Grace had first arrived in Cheapside the so-called memories that she had trotted out to support her claim had all been based on the kind of details that Joel could have found out and passed on to her without any difficulty. She knew, for instance, that her alleged foster-mother had red hair. This was the sort of information that Joel could have drawn out of Mrs. Tabor herself, or one of her servants, without their ever being conscious of it. But there seemed to be no way in which either Joel or Grace could have acquired the golden house rhyme to use as a proof of her identity. And in any case that was not how Grace had used it. All her other memories, true or spurious, had been related with great conviction as though they were matters of enormous import. The rhyme had been merely told to the children and overheard by accident. Which was an overwhelming point in her favour.

Philadelphia was faced with the conclusion that Grace must be Frances Tabor after all.

Then what about the suggestion that she had been at the Charity Hospital long before she was five years old? It was based, after all, on a passing remark that might easily have been misunderstood . . . Philadelphia felt thankful that she had never got to the point of repeating her suspicions to Laurence. It was the only consolation she could find in the history of her encounters with that insufferable young man.

20

MRS. TABOR was delighted with the new evidence that made Grace almost certainly her grand-daughter. The Beck sisters were good-naturedly pleased. Philadelphia was puzzled.

And Grace was absolutely thunder-struck. It was some time before she could take in exactly what had happened, and when she understood, she could scarcely believe it. She had produced, out of her own experience of the past, a little scrap of knowledge that could only have belonged to someone closely connected with the Tabor family.

This was so extraordinary that she hardly knew how to contain her astonishment, and had to keep very quiet to avoid seeming too much surprised, for she was faced with a situation that no one else suspected. To the others in the house she had to be either the real Frances Tabor, or an impostor. Grace alone knew that Joel had taught her all the rest of her part but not the golden rhyme. She could not think where it had come from; she had certainly known it long before she ever met Joel. Unlike her other pretended memories, it was a true fragment of her childhood.

After the first bewilderment she began to see that there was a way — the only way, surely — in which she could have heard that verse. All the rhymes and singing games they used at the Charity Hospital were a common heritage passed on by the older children to the younger; some no doubt had come originally from Mrs. Bullace, but many had been brought in by those children who had come to the Hospital when they were already able to speak — children who had once had proper homes and families to care for them. At five years old, Frances Tabor would have been such a child. Joel had actually traced her to the Hospital and although Mrs. Bullace said she had never been admitted there, it now appeared to Grace that Mrs. Bullace must have been wrong.

Grace started wondering which of the

other girls might have been Frances. There were around forty children, boys and girls, at the Hospital, most of whom arrived as unwanted babies and stayed till they were put out to work at twelve or thirteen; there were never more than a handful at any one age. It was true that ages were sometimes confused in a place where birthdays were generally unknown, but it was not possible to go very far wrong, and Grace felt sure that Frances could only be looked for among the girls who had been very little older or younger than herself.

She passed them all in front of her mind's eye. Most of them had left the Hospital before her, a few had been adopted, one or two had died, but she had forgotten none of them. When you lived in such a small worked, you did not overlook any of the inhabitants.

None of them seemed right for Frances. Her friend Nan wouldn't do; lucky Nan had a father who took her away to live with him. And Bess Barnsley had a mother who used to come to the Hospital and shout lewd insults at Mrs. Bullace when she was drunk.

What about one of the two Megs? Fat Meg had a brother in the boys' part of the Hospital, they had lived with their grandmother until she died. And Thin Meg, who was at least a foundling, had come to the Hospital even earlier than Grace, and long before Frances. That was the trouble: the nameless foundlings had all arrived at the Hospital too young, and when older children were admitted, everyone knew who they were.

Grace went over and over the names in her head, and not one of them would do.

It had stopped raining, and after supper she went for a walk in the garden, accompanied by her friend the stable cat. She had come to the conclusion that she herself was the real Frances Tabor.

She had always believed until now that she had been brought up in the Hospital from her infancy, but it was only what other people had told her, she had no definite recollection of where she had spent her earliest years, and of all the possible candidates she herself was the most likely, if only she could slough off the skin of Grace Wilton, who had been in Southwark since she was a baby. Perhaps the real Grace had died and the name had been passed on . . . She was not greatly interested in working out the details, being far more curious to find out whether she could, in fact, remember anything very early in her life that did not fit into the pattern of the Charity Hospital.

She dredged as deep as she could, with her eyes tight shut. At first there was nothing but a series of familiar images, and then — yes, there had been a flicker of a different scene, very slight and so far back in time that you could not call it a memory; it was rather the consciousness of having once remembered something that had now gone. She was aware of herself, as a child, trying to re-live a journey in a hay wagon. There was some connection with the river and a lot of boats — the strangeness of seeing those boats for the first time, was that it? And the wagon had come from a place called Milstock. She knew this quite suddenly and without question. Joel had told her that Milstock in Kent was a village where little Frances had lived with her foster-parents. The place had meant nothing to her then. It was a new, colourless name that failed to evoke the Milstock which had been buried deep in her mind, along with the hay wagon, many years ago.

She was convinced that she had just remembered her arrival in Southwark with her foster-parents when she was five years old.

21

IT was oppressively hot in Cheapside, with every hint of a breeze blocked out by the tall houses, and the pervasive market smells of sour milk and rotting vegetables. Joel, sweating in the workshop, found that his mind kept slipping off to Hertfordshire, and not just because he would have liked a sight of leafy trees and clear water. He was always thinking about Grace these days; it was strange how much he missed her about the house — that simple, ignorant little girl whom he had once considered merely as a pawn in his own game. Now he was haunted by the echo of her gentle voice, her wide-eyed, childish delight in anything that was new to an unspoilt mind. He could see her face half-hidden by the shining veil of hair, and remember what it felt like when he held her in his arms. Here he always stopped, miserably ashamed of the way he had treated her. How could he have been such a brute? He longed to be able to tell her he was sorry and to assure her that he would never hurt her in any way — but while she was down at Thurley he had no means of getting in touch with her.

Laurence went down there several times during August and September; unfortunately Laurence was not the best person to ask about Grace.

The two men had little to say to each other; Laurence was always just and punctilious in his dealings with Joel, but he kept an icy distance between them. He was very different with the other journeymen and apprentices; he was giving Sam drawing lessons.

Sam, boylike, was dazzled by his new hero, and quoted his words of wisdom as though no one had ever tried to teach him anything before. This was very natural, and Joel told himself constantly that it was wrong to be jealous of Laurence for taking Sam away from his family. Eventually it dawned on him that he didn't envy Laurence his ascendancy over Sam; he envied Sam the privilege of being Laurence's pupil.

He kept this shocking discovery to himself, and Laurence certainly had no inkling of it. In due course he went away again, not to Thurley this time, but to Bristol.

"Heaven knows what he wanted to go there for," grumbled Mr. Zachary. "All this traipsing around, when he ought to stay at home and nurse the shop — this isn't the way things were done in his uncle's day."

Joel listened with a mixture of amusement and irritation. Fond as he was of his father, he privately acknowledged that the old man was out of his depth these days. Having accepted Laurence as the lawful heir, promoted over his head, he had entirely failed to see what a remarkably gifted craftsman their new master was. He admitted that his jewels were excellently contrived, but did not admire them or believe that they would sell. Even when the shop was full of prosperous and discerning customers he suspected that they were idle profligates, unable to pay their bills.

"Laurence might at least have given me

some warning." Mr. Downes continued his monologue. "There's the coach to be ordered for Thurley . . . "

"Is Gra — is Miss Tabor coming home?"

"Not yet; it's the nieces and their families. Laurence forgot to tell me how many maidservants they have with them, or how much baggage; I don't know whether to order an extra cart or a couple of packhorses; how am I supposed to guess what they will require?"

In spite of these difficulties, the two Beck daughters and their entourage were safely brought back to London, and the morning after they arrived Joan Bradshaw came round to the shop with a letter for Laurence from his aunt. Joel was serving two customers at the time, she gave him a friendly wave in passing, and he strained his ears to hear what she was saying to her brother Edmund.

"She wanted Laurence to know at once . . . fresh evidence . . . a rhyme we knew in the nursery . . . must recognise her as Frank's daughter now."

Fresh evidence? What on earth were they talking about?

"Haven't you anything more to show us?" demanded Joel's customer, a provincial worthy, as fat as a bag-pudding, who was spending a lot of money on a gaudy young woman who certainly wasn't his wife.

Joel brought out several more pieces of plate, his attention still tuned to the tantalising scraps of conversation that came from the other side of the shop.

'Golden apples and silver pears . . . Uncle William Tabor . . . Cicely Fox . . . '

"What's the picture on this dish?" asked the young courtesan.

Joel took a closer look. "It's a Biblical subject, madam."

He thought she might not care to be told that it was the Parable of the Wise Virgins. Should he try to sell them that bowl with the engraving of Danaë receiving the shower of gold? They were probably too stupid to see the insult. If only they would go away!

At last they did go, and he was able to join Edmund and Joan, who related in chorus the extraordinary story of Grace and the family rhyme.

"Strange that this should happen just now," added Edmund.

"Why?" asked his sister.

"Because Laurence went to Bristol to look for a witness who he said might settle Grace's pretensions for good. Well, it was meant to be a secret, but I don't suppose it matters now." Edmund picked up Mrs. Tabor's letter. "I'll take care of this, but the chances are my aunt will be seeing Laurence before he ever reads it. I think he means to go straight back to Thurley."

Joel spent the rest of that day in a state of growing alarm. First there was this rhyme of Grace's which had achieved such magical results; he didn't know where she had got hold of it, but he felt sure she would soon be found out. It was a fatal mistake for her to have started producing evidence, she hadn't the guile to carry through such a deception on her own. Far more sinister was the news about Laurence. What sort of a witness could he have gone to find in Bristol? Could he have broken the deadlock which Joel himself had considered insoluble — discovered someone who knew what had happened to the real Frances after the death of her foster-parents at the Rose of York tavern? In that case, the fat really would be in the fire.

He spent an uneasy night, haunted by the thought of that silly little innocent down at Thurley imagining she'd been so clever, and of Laurence going there to confront her. She would have no one to advise or defend her, she would be utterly terrified.

He went to the shop next morning, but could not settle for thinking of Grace. Presently he escaped from the house by way of the workshop, crossed the patch of garden, and opened a small door leading into an alley-way which ran along the back of Goldsmiths' Row between Bread Street and Bow Lane. As he stepped through, he bumped into a hefty, broad-shouldered boy with a thatch of fair hair, who was just coming in.

"What do you want?" asked Joel. It was the servants' entrance, but this boy didn't look like a household servant, he was not delivering or selling anything, nor was he dressed as an apprentice. Hard to say what he was.

"I've come to see Grace. Mrs. Grace Tabor."

"Well, you won't find her; she's in Hertfordshire."

"That's a lie!" said the boy, suddenly belligerent. "She came home yesterday, so don't try to put me off with any of your lies, Master Joel Downes!"

"How do you know my name? And who the devil are you?" He studied the strange boy more closely. "I have it; you must be the young — stone-mason, is it? Her friend from the Charity Hospital. What is it she calls you — Coney?"

"Yes, I'm Coney, and I know she came home yesterday, for I met one of the fellows that went with the coach."

"You are mistaken; it was two of Mrs. Tabor's nieces that returned yesterday. I swear that's the truth," he added, seeing Coney's expression of stubborn mistrust. And then, as an afterthought: "What is it to you, anyway? You've been told to keep away from her."

"The old woman warned me off, yes. I reckon I can take my chance of being caught. But don't think I'm afraid of you, there's nothing you dare do to stop me seeing Grace — when she does come back. I know too much about your plotting with Mrs. Bullace . . . "

"For heaven's sake, hold your tongue!" Joel glanced round anxiously, but luckily there was no one about, the lane was deserted.

"And all those lies you forced Grace to tell," continued Coney implacably.

"There was no need of force," sid Joel, stung. "She was perfectly willing. And from what I hear, she has now taken to inventing stories on her own account."

"What do you mean?"

"I'm told she has started remembering matters that were supposed to be unknown outside the Tabor family."

"Do they believe her?"

"Apparently."

"Then she's safe enough," said Coney, coming off his high ethical perch. "It's when people get angry with her that she's liable to break down and confess. She never could withstand unkindness."

"I know," admitted Joel gloomily, "and

I fear that her courage may shortly be put to the test."

"So what are you doing about it? Making off while the going's good?"

"No, I am not! I was on my way to the stables, if you must know, to see whether I could hire a horse and ride down to Hertfordshire."

"Will you take me with you?"

"You? No, why should I? There's nothing you can do."

There was probably nothing anyone could do. He was going with no set plan, because he had no exact knowledge of the danger. To run away from a threat that didn't exist would be as disastrous as staying to brazen out Laurence's accusations and failing. His real reason for going to Thurley was to stand by Grace, whatever happened, and whether he could protect her or not. It was nothing to do with Coney — though it struck him that Grace needed some other friend besides himself, and he had no right to deprive her of the only one she had.

"Let me come with you," persisted the boy. "I won't be any trouble."

Joel hesitated. "I can't afford to hire a second horse, even if you could ride one, which I'm sure you can't."

"You can take me up behind you. Otherwise I'll walk the whole way."

22

GRACE and Philadelphia had persuaded Mrs. Tabor to take a walk in the demesne, so that she could see the improvements that Laurence was going to make that autumn. It was a warm afternoon, which was just as well; walking with Mrs. Tabor was like going on progress with a snail. She enjoyed seeing everything and having it explained to her by Philadelphia, but she was rather short of breath and she suffered with her feet.

As they strolled back to the house, they were surprised to see some strange horses being led off towards the stables, one of them carrying a side-saddle.

"Whoever can have come visiting at such an hour?" wondered Mrs. Tabor.

The steward, hovering in the hall, informed them that his master had arrived, unannounced and bringing a guest with him. It was clear that he was deeply incensed and would have said a lot more, but fortunately Laurence himself came downstairs at this moment to greet them.

"My dear boy!" exclaimed his aunt. "Did you get my letter with the good news about Grace?"

"I've had no letters, madam. Where did you send it?"

"Why, to Cheapside. Joan took it with her when they returned to the City . . ."

"Ah, but I haven't come from the City. I've been down to the West Country, and I've brought back a guest who's waiting in the gallery to meet you."

He marshalled them skilfully up the staircase, without answering any of Mrs. Tabor's questions.

"Who do you think it can be?" whispered Grace.

Philadelphia shook her head.

When they entered the gallery they saw a woman in a red dress sitting by the chimney-piece at the far end. She got up and came towards them. Grace immediately wondered if Laurence had discovered a rival claimant, another girl pretending to be Frances. She heard

Philadelphia catch her breath; perhaps she thought the same.

But the stranger was not a young girl, she was a woman of over thirty, plump and pretty. An amazing thought flashed through Grace's mind. Could this be my mother? Suppose she didn't die, after all?

Only this woman had black hair and brown eyes, and though Mrs. Tabor had given a little cry of astonishment she was not unduly put out.

"I need not present Mrs. Iredale to you," said Laurence, "for you recognise her, don't you?"

"It's Bess!" exclaimed Mrs. Tabor. "Bess Angell! Oh, my dear, how glad I am to see you again, after so many years."

"Nearly half my lifetime, madam," said the dark woman. "I'm flattered you knew me so quickly."

They embraced, and Grace looked curiously at Mrs. Iredale, the friend who had sheltered Frank and sent Mrs. Tabor the news of her death.

The two women had not met since, as they were reminding each other now.

"Your family sent you away in disgrace, and there were many questions I was not able to ask you — but that's of no account, for we have answered the most important question of all. We have recovered my grand-daughter — and here she is!" announced Mrs. Tabor, proudly indicating Grace.

"Well, as to that, madam, I fear you may be mistaken," said Bess Iredale. She sounded regretful and uneasy.

"But why should you think that?" demanded Mrs. Tabor.

Why indeed? She hardly looked at me, thought Grace. How could she tell whether or not I was the baby she saw nearly sixteen years ago?

Yet here she was, saying firmly: "I'm afraid this cannot be your grandchild, madam."

"I assure you, we have proof . . . "

"Mrs. Tabor, pray listen to me! When I wrote you that letter, just after Frank's death, I was in great distress and confusion of mind, besides being a very poor hand with a pen, and totally unversed in breaking bad news. So that's how it came about — though when Laurence quoted my own words back to me, I could scarcely believe that I had been such a fool. There was one circumstance I failed to make plain, relating to the baby . . . "

"Did the baby die also?" interrupted Philadelphia. "Is that what you are trying to tell us? Or was she deformed in some way?"

"No, not that." Bess Iredale took a deep breath. "I am very sorry, Mrs. Tabor, and I hope you will be able to forgive me. It seems that I have unwittingly misled you for the past fifteen years. Frank's child was a boy."

23

FOR a moment they were stunned into immobility. Then there was an uproar of questions and answers — Bess had simply given the child's Christian name, said Laurence, forgetting it was the one name that could be used for either a boy or a girl. And Mrs. Tabor, thinking of the daughter she had lost, immediately jumped to the conclusion that the child who had survived her was a daughter.

She wasn't ready to give up that conclusion; she collapsed into a flood of tears, and the more they tried to reason with her, the more hysterical she became. Laurence supported his afflicted aunt, while Bess Iredale untied her laces, and Philadelphia ran to fetch a pitcher of water. There was a general commotion, some of the servants came to see what was wrong, headed by Mr. Simeon Wacey, hovering like a vulture.

Grace was incredulous. Ten days ago

she had found an answer to the riddle of her own existence, she had established herself as a real person, with roots that went deeper than the thin soil of the Charity Hospital. And now they were saying that the young girl called Frances Tabor was a myth. It was a wicked falsehood.

"She wasn't a boy," Grace burst out passionately. "She was a girl, she must have been, because I'm Frances. I can remember all those things, the cottage at Milstock and the hay wagon. And the rhyme. If I'm not Frances, how did I come to know the rhyme?"

"I suppose you were taught it by Joel, as you were taught everything else," snapped Philadelphia. "I guessed how it was, when I caught you out in a lie two months ago, only I was fool enough to keep quiet."

"It's not true," protested Grace. "Joel didn't teach me the rhyme, I swear he didn't. I've known it all my life."

"Oh, for God's sake hold your tongue and get out of my way. You've done enough harm already."

Philadelphia turned distractedly to

Mrs. Tabor, who seemed to be having a kind of spasm. Grace watched her for a moment, and then tiptoed out of the gallery.

She took refuge in her bedchamber while she tried to understand what was happening, and how it was that she felt herself to be inhabiting the body and mind and memory of a girl who apparently didn't exist. She could see that cottage in Kent — well, not see it exactly, but she knew it was there. With a quince tree in the garden, and a dog called Punch.

She brooded over this mystery for some time, but she could make no headway, and presently other thoughts took hold. Philadelphia had sounded so angry, accusing her of lying, and of course all those other stories *had* been lies. Which meant that no one would believe anything else she said, even when it was true. What would they do to her? She thought of the kind of treatment she would get from Mr. Tucker, though even that would not be as bad as the things they could do to you in prison. She was a thief, wasn't she? And suppose poor Mrs.

Tabor were to die, she had looked a very alarming purple colour out there in the gallery. "Then I should be a murderer," wailed Grace, halfway between panic and remorse.

Presently one of the chambermaids appeared, saying that the master had sent for her.

"Is my gra — is Mrs. Tabor recovered?" asked Grace fearfully.

"Small thanks to you if she is," said the woman, whose name was Gertrude. She was a sour, uncomfortable person, and like so many of the Thurley hangers-on, an indigent relative of Mr. Wacey. She conducted Grace down the back stairs.

Grace was too miserable to wonder why she was being taken into the servants' quarters. She was just beginning to think this was rather odd when Gertrude opened the door of one of the bick-flagged rooms behind the buttery and pushed her inside.

She came to a halt, facing a group of eight people who were all staring expectantly towards the door. There was Temperance, another chambermaid; she was a widow with a simple-minded son and a daughter who suffered from the falling sickness. They were there too. There was also an old retired servitor called Orliss, and at the back, leaning against the wall, three stable-boys, low persons who were not usually admitted to the house. Seated in the centre, like a judge, was Mr. Simeon Wacey.

"Where's Mr. Laurence?" Grace appealed to Gertrude. "Why have you brought me here?"

"We wish to examine you concerning your crimes," declared the steward.

"I accuse her!" The widow Temperance shot out a pointing finger. "I accuse her of the vile and abominable sin of witchcraft. She cast a spell on my unhappy daughter so that she fell into a fit many times more violent than ever before . . . "

"Witchcraft!" repeated Grace, turning pale with fright. "I don't know what you mean, I never had any traffic in such things. Sir, I beg you to believe me!"

It was the most terrifying charge that could be brought against anyone.

"There is evidence that you used satanic arts to satisfy your evil ambitions," said Wacey.

"What evidence? There must be a mistake."

"You have claimed to know things you could not have learnt in any ordinary manner. How did you learn that rhyme?"

Since Grace did not know the answer herself, she shook her head dumbly. She was trembling so that she could hardly stand, and there was so much hostility directed towards her, in that small space, it was like a physical impact. She tried to back away from Wacey, but Gertrude was behind her, blocking the door.

"Answer me, slut," said the steward. "Who taught you the rhyme?"

"I — don't know."

"There" said Gertrude triumphantly. "What did I tell you? She's a witch."

The others all began to agree. Grace looked anxiously from face to face, hope dying away as she saw in each one the same irrational hatred and mounting excitement. All those inbred monsters were intoxicated with their own power. Only old Orliss said grudgingly that they had better be careful in case the wench was madam's grandchild after all.

"Why, do you think she's a man?"

asked one of the stable-boys. "Give her to me then, and I warrant I'll find out."

"This is no time for levity," said Wacey. "You were allowed in here on sufferance because you had some further charge to make."

"She has a familiar spirit," put in a second stable-boy. "A cat that jumps on her shoulder when she walks alone in the garden at night."

"Does she fondle it and speak to it as though it was her paramour?" asked Temperance eagerly.

"Ay, mistress. She does just that."

This caused a sensation. The youngest stable-boy said perhaps she was fond of cats, but no one paid any attention to him. Gertrude made a more practical suggestion.

"We could strip her to see whether she has a third nipple."

"Oh, no!" whispered Grace, shrinking away.

It was a well-known fact that a witch often had this third nipple in order to suckle her familiar. Grace had no mole or blemish anywhere on her body, but the thought of being pawed and peered at by this obscene crew filled her with revulsion.

Wacey had a different test for her. Let her recite the Lord's Prayer from beginning to end without faltering.

Grace tried to do as she was told. In fact she was praying harder and more fervently then she had ever prayed before, but whether it was her bad conscience or simply her acute nervousness, she stumbled over the word trespasses, and everything else was lost in a howl of execration. This showed that she was in league with the devil.

An argument now started between the servants, some saying that they ought to take her before a magistrate, others that they needed one more definite demonstration to clinch the matter. Grace did not follow what they were saying; by this time she had been driven stupid with fear and hardly knew what was going on. Impressions came to her in waves — ugly faces, cruel voices — she was imprisoned in a world of nightmare; she had virtually forgotten that Mrs. Tabor and Laurence and Philadelphia were somewhere in the same building. No one would hear her if she cried out, there was no one she could ask for help.

Someone said that swimming a witch was the soundest proof of all. Old-fashioned, but the old ways were the best.

Grace found she was being taken out of the house. They muffled her head in a cloak, to keep her from making a noise, and the men bundled her along between them, half lifting, half dragging her. She could see nothing, because of the stifling cloak; she was pinched and bruised and she kept twisting her ankles.

They were crossing the rough grass, there was a hubbub all round her, but she still did not know where she was until someone pulled off the cloak, and she found herself standing at the edge of the lake.

The evening was misty, the water had a cold, secret, unfriendly look; it was stagnant and covered with weeds. She gaped at it, uncomprehending, while Wacey portentously explained the custom of swimming a witch. The suspect was thrown into deep water; if she sank, she was innocent. If she floated, she was

271

guilty and would suffer the penalty for witchcraft.

"No!" sobbed Grace, sick with terror. "No! No! No!"

She struggled frantically to escape, but she was surrounded. The youngest stable-boy said he couldn't see any sense in drowning the poor girl to see if she was innocent. Everyone else was engaged in tying Grace's hands behind her back so that see couldn't save herself.

They swung her off her feet and plunged her as far out into the lake as they could manage. She fell with a flat splash, shutting her eyes and holding her breath, certain that she was going to drown. Once her head went under she would be finished.

Her skirt fanned out and was caught in the web of weeds, so that she was suspended on the surface of the water.

A shout went up from the bank. "She's floating! She's possessed by the devil! Have her out and we can deal with her!"

Grace began to scream.

24

PHILADELPHIA helped Mrs. Tabor to undress and got her into bed. The old woman was calmer now, sad and defeated.

"I shouldn't have tried to find the child," she said. "I suppose I was asking to be cozened out of my money — that's how John would have seen it. But I so longed to have a grand-daughter, I thought she would be like Frank come to life once more. And that was foolishness; my Frank's dead, and I shall never see her again in this world."

Philadelphia comforted her as best she could. This unusual clarity, she thought, must be the result of a simple mind being painfully confronted with the truth. Mrs. Tabor was often very silly; just now she had achieved a certain tragic dignity.

She persuaded her mistress to swallow an opiate draught, but even before it had time to work, Mrs. Tabor had fallen asleep from sheer exhaustion.

Philadelphia gently pulled the curtains round the bed. She discovered that she was very tired. She wondered whether she ought to go and find Grace, but decided to let her stew a little longer. She was angry, not merely with Grace, but with herself for failing to pass on her suspicions to Laurence. She knew why she had failed; her contradictory feelings for him had got in the way. It was humiliating.

She found him with Mrs. Iredale in the gallery.

"How is my aunt?" he asked.

"She's gone off to sleep and I think the worst is over. I believe you will find her more reasonable in the morning."

"I blame myself for breaking the news in such a way. The fact is, I lured Mrs. Iredale over here to put this matter straight, and she can't stay with us long. Her husband's away at sea, and she's greatly needed at home."

"Besides which," said Bess Iredale, "I doubt if Mrs. Tabor would have been able to accept the news I brought unless it had been forced down her throat. She has been dreaming of a grand-daughter for so many years — what a fool I was when I wrote that letter!"

She sounded contrite, though she looked a cheerful and resilient little person; one who would feel her troubles acutely but soon recover.

Philadelphia glanced from Bess to Laurence, and several facts fell into place. "You've known all along, haven't you? That your cousin's child was a boy?"

"Yes."

"Then why, in heaven's name, didn't you say so when you first came home?"

"It's a long story."

He paused and she sat down in the window-seat beside Bess, prepared to listen.

"When we were all young," he said, "my greatest friend was Mrs. Iredale's brother Tom. We were three years younger than her and Frank, and of course we knew, as children always do, a great deal more than our elders suppose. After Frances vanished from Goldsmiths' Row her name was never spoken, but I knew perfectly well that she'd run away with Robin Martel. I knew when she died, though that wasn't mentioned either. I dare say you've been told that Bess was immediately packed off to her kinsfolk in Somerset, because of the disgrace she'd got into through helping my cousin. However, Tom saw her at Enfield before she left, and he told me, as a deadly secret, that Frank had given birth to a son.

"Well, it was a nine days' wonder to us both, and Frank's death was a great sorrow, but as for her child, I can't say I was much occupied in thinking of him. Boys don't care for infants in their cradles. Tom and I believed that my uncle would provide for him, but we knew better than to raise the subject with our families, and as time went on I practically forgot his existence.

"Until I came home this spring, and you presented Grace to me as Frank's long-lost daughter."

"And you took me for an impudent adventuress," said Philadelphia sweetly. "I'm beginning to see why."

Laurence flushed. "I was so astonished that I misjudged your place in the scheme of things — but only for a very short time. I thought, you see, that Grace must have been introduced into the house by someone so ignorant of our family history that they didn't even know the one fact that should have been beyond question — the sex of my cousin's child.

"I was even more astonished to learn that it was Mrs. Tabor herself who had set on foot the search for her supposed grand-daughter. She told me she had certain knowledge of the girl's existence from a letter Bess had written her the day Frank died."

"Did she show you the letter?"

"Not then. If she had, I should have acted differently. As it was, I decided that either Tom had been mistaken, or that my own memory had played me false. What would you believe in such a case? The written testimony of an eyewitness, or a whisper of forbidden gossip passed between two boys of fourteen?"

"You should have known better than to trust this eyewitness," said Bess Iredale ruefully.

"I should have known better than to trust my poor aunt," he retorted. "However, I accepted the news that my illegitimate cousin was a girl, not a boy, though I never accepted Grace as the rightful claimant. There was something — I don't know how to describe it — when I first rejected her, simply because she wasn't a boy, she seemed at once too much afraid and too little surprised. And I was certain Joel was in league with that woman at the Charity Hospital, they were both far too glib. So I went on arguing with my aunt, and eventually she showed me Bess's famous letter."

"So you discovered you'd been right all along."

"No, I didn't. That's the crux of the whole matter. I discovered that was equal chances, boy or girl, we had no proof either way."

"Surely the church register at Enfield . . . "

"There was no entry. Remember that Bess baptised the child the day it was born. And the midwife is now an old woman who has delivered to many babies that she can't remember any of them clearly. I myself had now decided that what Tom had told me was true, but do you think my aunt would have accepted that scrap of hearsay evidence, after those years of convincing herself that somewhere in the world she had a beautiful, fair-haired grand-daughter, the image of Frank?"

"No," said Philadelphia, "I see your dilemma. You had to have something more solid to go on. So you decided to find Mrs. Iredale?"

"You must understand," he said, "that I thought it would be easy, that I simply had to discover through the assay-master where Tom was working now; he would tell me where to look for Bess, and we should get the thing decided with hardly any delay. That was why I continued to hold my tongue."

The assay-master, thought Philadelphia. Of course, Tom Angell was a goldsmith too, so he was probably practising his craft somewhere in the provinces. Because of the need to ensure that precious metals were sold at their proper weight and value, the Goldsmiths' Company of London had a certain authority over all the goldsmiths and silversmiths in the kingdom, and their assay-master went on tours of inspection at regular intervals. A man of Laurence's standing should have had no trouble in locating his friend. Yet something must have gone wrong. Perhaps Tom Angell was dead? She looked enquiringly at his sister.

"My brother went to Bristol," she said, "after my father was sold up. He married the daughter of a merchant captain, and found a sea-faring life suited him better than the anvil or the shop. A strange choice, but it's brought him prosperity. And I married his partner, I'm afraid we have been a sad trial to Laurence."

He had almost given up hope of tracing them, and then, while he was down here at Thurley, it came out by chance that one of the neighbouring squires had a sister who still kept in touch with some of the Angell family. In due course Laurence was able to get news of Bess. He had gone tearing down to Bristol to enlist her help. She was delighted to see him but rather surprised by his mission. Of course she had told Mrs. Tabor that the child was a boy. Laurence had quoted her own letter to her (he now knew it by heart) and Bess was appalled. She offered to come and put things right, and they had ridden straight to Thurley.

So much was now made plain, especially Laurence's flat refusal to accept Grace as his cousin, right from the start, before he had made the faintest attempt to examine the evidence. It was this high-handed attitude which had led Philadelphia to condemn him for being unjust, avaricious and heartless. Now, of course, she recognised the fact that had been literally staring him in the face. No wonder he had been so definite. And in the end he had been proved right. Was that entirely a cause for satisfaction? He had destroyed an illusion that was making his aunt happy without doing her any particular harm. Couldn't he have left well alone? No, Philadelphia decided after a moment's reflection, he could not allow that foolish and vulnerable old woman to be deceived. He had to speak out, any man of integrity would have felt the same.

"There's one thing I don't understand," she said thoughtfully.

"Only one?"

"One will do to start with. How was it, when Joel went to look for the missing grandchild down in Kent, that he didn't discover it was a boy?"

"I don't suppose Joel went any further than Southwark. I suspect he made straight for the Charity Hospital and chose a pretty, docile girl who would do exactly as she was bid. I dare say he meant to marry her, once her inheritance seemed secure."

"Oh. I had not considered — do you think Mr. Zachary Downes is in the plot?"

"I'm certain he is not."

"Yet you are determined to believe the worst of Joel?"

"Far from it," he said with unexpected vehemence. "You don't know how awkwardly I am placed."

Philadelphia was wondering what to make of this cryptic statement, when Bess turned her head slightly and said, "Listen!"

There were distant sounds and cries coming from the garden. They all looked out of the window on to a map-like view of desiccated flower beds, overgrown hedges and cropped grass spreading down to the lake. There were seven or eight people moving about and waving their arms at the water's edge; the autumn evening had thrown up a layer of mist, and it was hard to tell what they were doing.

"Isn't that your steward?" asked Bess. "I can't see why — look, they've got something in the water."

"It's a woman," said Laurence. "My God, it's Grace!"

He wasted no more time. He was across the gallery and half-way down the stairs before Philadelphia had properly taken in what was happening. She and Bess ran after him, as fast as they could in their heavy skirts, out of the front door and into the forecourt; he had already vanished when they rounded the side of the house. At last they emerged on to the grass. Laurence was still running, about twenty yards ahead of them, and some sort of fight had started beside the lake. They could no longer see Grace, she was hidden from them by the level of the bank, but they could hear her crying out for help, and Philadelphia, gasping for breath, could still see in her mind's eye, the horrifying vision of a white-faced doll bobbing in the water, with her hair streaming around her.

A sudden bulk loomed out of the mist: a horse, wearily grazing, with a saddle on its back and reins dragging on the ground. She did not stop to wonder what it was doing there.

Laurence had now reached the party on the bank. The fight was unevenly matched, there were four men against one, and they had got him down on the ground and were kicking and hitting him with sticks, cheered on by an older man and several women. There was a babel of noise, but the screams from the lake had stopped.

Laurence sailed straight in to the mêleé, seized Simeon Wacey by his black coat, swung him round and gave him a cracking blow on the jaw. Wacey went down like a stone. Laurence planted himself in front of the injured man and sent another of his assailants flying. The two remaining warriors ran away. A fat woman in an apron went chasing after one of them with little cries of concern. Philadelphia recognised Temperance, the chambermaid, and her imbecile son. She also recognised, with a kind of unrelated astonishment, that the man on the grass was Joel.

She could think of nothing but Grace and that ominous silence after the screaming. As the edge of the lake became visible, her heart gave a plunge of relief, for there were two other figures down there with Grace, supporting her between them: a young urchin who worked in the stables, and a fair-haired boy whom she had never seen before. They were standing waist-deep in water, their hands green with slime, as they tried to lift Grace clear of the reeds, and the stranger was comforting her as though he had known her all her life.

25

ONE of the most extraordinary facts of that extraordinary evening was that Mrs. Tabor slept through everything. Going up for the third time to make sure that she was comfortable, Philadelphia was thankful to find that she had not moved an inch. She reckoned it was a dispensation of Providence.

There had been so much to do when they got back to the house. Grace had to be revived and comforted and helped into dry clothes — she would not go to bed because she was afraid of being left alone: she clung to the strange boy who had arrived so mysteriously with Joel and rescued her from the lake. As soon as Philadelphia heard her calling him Coney one half of the mystery was solved. The other half, the question of what they were doing at Thurley, would have to wait. Philadelphia had found clothes for Coney too, and for the small stable-boy who had bravely taken Grace's part, and who had now been sent home to his family with much praise and commendation.

Joel, unlike the other three, had not been in the lake, but he needed the most attention. He had managed to hold back Wacey and his minions while Coney jumped into the water to rescue Grace, and in doing so he had been severely beaten, his body was covered with gashes and bruises, especially his arms, legs and ribs; he had a black eye and a cut mouth. Philadelphia and Bess had dressed his wounds, while the depleted household servants brought in a makeshift supper and prepared a bedchamber for the unexpected guests.

As she crossed the dark hall, Philadelphia could see through the open doorway into the parlour, the people inside held within its frame, like actors on a stage. Grace was sitting on a tuffet, drying her long hair in front of the wood fire. She was as pale as wax, and could not stop trembling; even so, she had survived her horrifying ordeal better than they had dared to hope. Coney sat cross-legged on the floor beside her, a tough, resilient, watchful boy, who undoubtedly saw himself as her only protector.

Laurence was still sitting at the end of the supper-table, only slightly ruffled by his part in the fight. Beside him, Bess Iredale, in her red dress, was cutting up a plate of meat for Joel. And there was Joel himself, propped in a chair full of cushions, battered and wretched.

The lurid marks on his face made him look like a clown, and his right arm was in a sling. He had hardly spoken since they helped him back into the house. There had been too much to contend with: his own injuries, the shock of what those brutes had done to Grace, the threat of ruin now that their conspiracy had been uncovered. And finally the news that he had gone to so much trouble merely to stage the impersonation of an heiress who had never existed. That was the last straw.

Laurence heard Philadelphia's footsteps. He got up and came out into the hall to meet her.

Seeing him at close quarters, she realised that he was a good deal shaken, under his habitual composure, and she

288

had a sudden feeling of compunction for the way she had frequently misjudged him in the past. Perhaps if she had been more conciliating, he might have told her his real reason for refusing to accept Grace as his cousin. But she'd been so set on championing Grace at the start — only to abandon the poor little wretch in the end, when she most needed help. I left her alone, she thought, and those brutes nearly murdered her.

"You must be worn out," said Laurence. "I'm afraid I've let you bear the brunt of all this troublesome business; I don't know what we should have done without you."

"Oh, it's nothing," she disclaimed. "in fact, I was just thinking I'd left undone all the things I ought to have done. If I'd been charitable enough to go and look for Grace, after she was shown up as an imposter, those devils would never have got hold of her . . . "

"If that makes you feel guilty, what do you suppose I'm feeling? I set off the charge which led to all this devastation."

"You could hardly ignore the fact that your aunt was being deceived."

"Oh yes, I can justify my actions," he said. "I've been a model of self-righteous seal; Hannah Beck couldn't have managed better. Which reminds me, how is my aunt?"

"Fast asleep."

"We must be thankful for small mercies. There is another matter I wanted to discuss with you, but not in there, in front of that poor child. Mrs. Whitethorn, why did they accuse her of witchcraft?"

"I think it was on account of the rhyme your father wrote for Frances."

"My father?" he repeated.

She told him the history of the rhyme itself, and the sensation that Grace had produced when she quoted it, quite casually, to the children; all the delighted acclamation which the servants must have overheard. And surely he remembered, that afternoon in the gallery, Grace insisting, against all the evidence, that she must be the Tabor grandchild "because she knew the rhyme."

"She learnt it from Joel."

"Then why does she herself look on it as some kind of proof?"

290

"Do you suspect her of witchcraft?"

"Good God, no! But surely this doesn't matter any longer? You know for certain now that Grace is an imposter."

"It matters to this extent," he said. "That unsavoury fellow Wavey tried to brand her with this vile accusation. I'd like to dismiss him from my service and charge him with assault, but if Grace is going to be the subject to unanswered riddles and rumours that no one can explain, it will be difficult to free her entirely from the imputation of witchcraft. The whole business might continue to hang over her like a sword of Damocles."

Philadelphia was startled. He had dealt most effectively with the witch-hunters; Wacey was groaning in his chamber, still half stunned, and conscious of nothing but his own discomfort. Those two vicious louts would spend the night locked in the stable. The small fry had retreated thankfully out of sight, there was no fight in them. But she saw Laurence's point; they were not likely to relinquish their savage and distorted view of Grace unless it could be openly challenged and made to appear ridiculous.

"What can we do?" she asked.

"Ask some questions."

They went back into the parlour; he took a stool near the fire, and said quietly, to Grace: "I'm very sorry my servants used you so abominably. Whatever treatment you might have expected, it was nothing like that."

Grace flushed scarlet and began to shake more than ever. On Laurence's other side, Joel pushed away the plate of meat he was toying with, and braced himself to sit a little straighter in his chair. There had been an illusion until now that they and Laurence were allies, with Wacey and his followers as the common enemy. But that could not continue, there had got to be a reckoning between the two conspirators who had been found out, and the representative of the wealthy family they had conspired to rob.

There was an uneasy pause, broken surprisingly by Coney, who spoke up in a clear, young voice a little roughened by nervousness.

"I hope you won't be hard on Grace,

sir. She didn't properly understand what she was doing, not to start with, and she didn't want to go on cheating the old dame, only she was afraid to confess. She wasn't going to touch the inheritance. And as for all the money that's been spent on her already: we'll pay it back, bit by bit — I promise we will. I — I'm Grace's betrothed husband, sir, and I don't earn a great deal at present, but I mean to marry her and take care of her as soon as I can."

Philadelphia thought of the clothes and presents that had been lavished on Grace, and of the pittance that this boy would get in wages from the Dutch stone-carver, and hoped that for once Laurence's spirit of mockery would remain dormant.

Laurence did not laugh. He said, "That is a great tribute. I hope you value it, Grace; I think it's more than you deserve."

"Oh yes, I do," she whispered, moving closer to Coney.

"That's the first I've heard of a betrothal," protested Joel.

"It's true, just the same," retorted Coney. "I didn't tell you on the ride down, or I dare say you'd have put me off that horse. And it's no concern of yours, all you ever did for Grace was to drag her into your plotting and teach her to do wrong, so that she was always in fear of discovery. When those villains threw her in the lake, it was all your fault."

"Yes, I know," whispered Joel, putting up a hand to shade his eyes. Philadelphia thought he was in a good deal of pain.

"Not all Joel's fault," remarked Laurence. "In this particular instance it's hard to say whose fault it was. I believe there is some question of a rhyme that you didn't get from Joel, is that so?

"No, I didn't." The mention of the rhyme had made Grace articulate. "I've known it all my life. The other things I did learn from Joel, but not that . . . If you please, Mr. Tabor — are you going to send me to prison?"

"No," he said gently, "you shan't go to prison."

"Or back to Southwark?"

"Southwark — good God! (No, my dear, you shan't go there either, don't fret.) "But I am just beginning to see — Joel, what was it took you to the Charity Hospital in the first place?"

"I followed your cousin's child right to the door, or so I thought."

"In which case I have done you an injustice."

Joel stared at him through bloodshot eyes. "It seems very unlikely," he said with a brave attempt at irony.

"I had never supposed that you made any effort to find my cousin. I thought you went straight to a place where you could get hold of a likely girl to satisfy my aunt."

"That's not true. I swear to you. I didn't set out to deceive her. Not until I had tried my hardest to discover the child. I always knew you suspected that part of the story; believe it or not, you were wrong."

"You have convinced me," said Laurence. "Frank's child must have been at the Charity Hospital at some time or another. How else did Grace learn the rhyme?"

"That's the part I can't fathom," said Joel slowly. "It doesn't make sense. Mrs.

Bullace assured me there never was a child at the Hospital who could have been your cousin."

"She was right, sir," put in Grace. "I've been thinking it over and over, and there isn't anyone who fits."

"Haven't you forgotten something?"

"What?"

"That you ought to have been looking for a boy."

"There was a moment's silence."

"Even so," said Joel, "it wouldn't have made any difference. I remember Mrs. Bullace saying that she had never admitted any unknown foundling who was past the age of infancy. She insisted that she knew the histories of all the older children committed to her care."

"Committed to her care? That's the point," said Laurence. "A boy of five would go straight into the Master's house, wouldn't he? Mrs. Bullace would hear all about him, I don't doubt, but he'd hardly enter into her calculation when she claimed that she knew where all her own particular children came from. And since you were looking for a girl, I don't suppose she'd even think to mention him

— why should she?"

"Oh!" said Grace, suddenly.

Laurence glanced at her. "Was there a boy who came to the Hospital when you were both around five years old? A boy who'd lived in the country, he may have told you stories as well as rhymes . . . "

"Yes," said Grace, her face full of wonder. "I ought to have guessed, all along. There was only one person it could ever have been. It was you that lived in the cottage, Coney, and came to Southwark in a farm wagon, riding on top of the hay . . . "

"What of it?" said Coney sharply. He was bewildered and defensive.

Laurence leant forward, scrutinising him closely. Philadelphia noticed with a flicker of excitement that the boy's capable, well-shaped hands were remarkably like his own.

"And your proper name is Francis," continued Grace, innocently stating a fact that she had taken for granted all along.

"What's that got to prove? It's the sort of name everyone has. There were two

Franks at the Hospital when I got there, you know that as well as I do. That's why I've always been Coney. And I can tell you one thing, sir," he added, addressing Laurence, "I've always known my proper surname, and it's not any of those they've been trying to fasten on Grace. It isn't Tabor or Fox or Perry."

"Is it by any chance Martel?"

Both the orphans gaped at him as though he was now the one who dealt in magic.

"How did you know?" breathed Grace.

"Because it was the only name left that Cicely Fox was likely to use if she didn't claim him as her own flesh and blood. Martel is your father's name, Francis. Even though you aren't entitled to use it, I dare say she hoped he might acknowledge you. That may be why she persuaded her husband to leave Kent and come to London, poor woman."

"I don't want anyone to acknowledge me," Coney had scrambled to his feet, angry and defiant. "I don't want to be a lapdog in any great family. I loved my nurse, she was the one who did everything for me. She told me I was the grandson of a lord, and my mother's family could buy up half London, but they never cared a straw for me, and I'll not go round whining to become their pensioner. I've got a craft of my own and I won't give it up to please anyone; I'm going to be an alabasterer and live the life I choose."

"Well done, Cousin Francis," said Laurence equably. "I know exactly how you feel."

Coney eyed him resentfully. "Don't you understand? I'm not your cousin, and I don't want to be."

"Very well." Laurence stood up. "I'd like a word with you in private, all the same."

"No," muttered Coney, childishly obstinate.

Laurence looked him up and down. "Cousin or no cousin, you're young enough to do as you're told," he said crisply.

Coney recognised the note of authority, and allowed himself to be shepherded out of the parlour.

In the shadowy hall, where he had consulted with Philadelphia, Laurence turned to his reluctant companion.

"Now," he said, not wasting words, "do you want to help Grace?"

"Why else should I be here?"

"Then listen to me. She's been accused of witchcraft because she seems to know things relating to the Tabor family which she can't account for and didn't get from Joel Downes. My steward has convinced himself that she's made a bargain with the devil. This is plain foolishness, but it's not easy to deny without some rational explanation. The fact is, of course, that she grew up alongside the child who had in truth been cared for by Cicely Fox. There's nothing strange about Grace knowing that rhyme; she heard it from you, and you heard it from Cicely, who was your mother's nurse. But if you refuse to let me say so, how can I clear Grace of that calumny?"

"I hadn't thought — I don't want her to suffer — you're not trying to trick me?" asked Coney with a return of suspicion.

"No, I promise you. Perhaps I should tell you that your grandfather tried very hard to prevent me becoming a painter.

Since I managed to get the better of him, it would be churlish of me to stop you following your chosen craft. You shall be a stone-carver — provided you're a good one. I warn you, I've no patience with bad workmen."

Coney grinned and said that he intended to be a very good stone-carver. Having overcome his distrust of Laurence, he was prepared to produce plenty of memories of Cicely Fox, and her stories about his parents. He had brought them all into the Charity Hospital, his only treasures, the fragments of a happier world. It was no wonder that Grace, with nothing of her own to recall, had brooded over everything he told her until it seemed to be part of her actual experience.

"Didn't it strike you," asked Laurence curiously, "that the child Grace was impersonating had a history extremely like your own?"

"No, for I never paid much attention. I hated her telling all those lies for money, and I wanted no part of it. Besides," Coney pointed out, "they were looking for a girl. How could I ever have guessed it was me they wanted?"

When they went back into the parlour, Laurence was able to inform the company that he was satisfied with Coney's credentials.

"This is Frank's son."

"I must say I should never have recognised you," said Bess Iredale, observing him carefully.

"Madam?"

Laurence laughed. "Mrs. Iredale is the only one of us you have previously met, Cousin. She christened you on the day you were born — in fact, I suppose she must be your godmother."

"Oh." The boy stood awkwardly on one leg and mumbled something inaudible.

"I should like to make up for lost time by doing some service, if I can, to help you," said Bess.

"I don't want . . . " began Coney, but Laurence pressed his arm, and he subsided.

"I was wondering," pursued Bess, "what is to become of Grace? Yes, I know you hope to marry in due course, but you're young to be thinking of that, you have your way still to make, and where's she to live in the meantime?"

No one felt qualified to answer. Grace was not to go to prison nor to the Charity Hospital (two fates she seemed to fear about equally) but it would hardly do for her to return to Goldsmiths' Row with Mrs. Tabor. The old woman was not vindictive, and might forgive her; even so, it would not be at all the same, and to make Grace go back, discredited, to a place where she had recently been shown off as an heiress — that would be turning kindness into a punishment.

The girl glanced from Laurence to Bess, her eyes full of wordless entreaty, like a lost dog.

"How would you like to come to Bristol with me, Grace, and help me to care for my children? There are six of them, three boys and three girls, and they are getting too much of a handful for my nursemaid. I should be glad of your company too, for my husband is so often away at sea."

"I'd like to go with you, madam," said Grace hesitantly. "I'd be happy to live in a house where there are young children to care for. If Mr. Tabor will allow me."

"Well, Laurence?"

Skilfully seizing his opportunity, Laurence set about breaking down his new-found cousin's last scruples of resistance.

"What do you say, Francis? I think this is as much your concern as mine."

"I'd be very glad for her to remain with Mrs. Iredale," said Coney in a splendidly grave and judicious manner. "She will be safe there. Until I can provide for her myself."

26

PHILADELPHIA was entrusted with the task of telling Mrs. Tabor that they had found her grandchild after all. Mrs. Tabor was pathetic and still half-drugged after a long night's sleep; she was not much interested in the news. If she had a strange grandson nearly sixteen years old, her only coherent feeling was that she did not want to see him.

This was in some ways a relief, otherwise Philadelphia would have been obliged to tell Coney's grandmother that he did not want to meet her.

"The case was different when I thought there was a girl," said the old woman after she had thought it over. "I wanted to find her. But I understand now that it was simply because I hoped she would remind me of Frank. So that I could enjoy the good times all over again, the years when we were happy, before she went away. I dare say that was wicked of me, grieving over the past — anyway,

I've learnt my lesson. You can't expect a child to play the part of its mother. And I don't understand these young creatures, I'm too old and too tired. I wish them both very well — Grace as well as Francis — I'm sure Laurence will do all that's required, and make proper provision — and one day, perhaps, he can bring the boy to see me. But not now."

So that was that. Mrs. Tabor did rouse herself, after some further meditation, to say that it seemed wrong for John's grandson to be lodging in the suburbs and earning his keep as the servant of an ignorant foreigner, instead of being properly apprenticed to a trade.

"Only consider, madam: Francis is past the age of starting an apprenticeship, so how fortunate it is that he has chosen a craft which he can practice without being a member of a company. Mr. Laurence is going to make certain that this Dutchman is a fit person to teach him; you need have no fear on that score."

"To be sure, that's a great comfort."

Mrs. Tabor relapsed amongst her

pillows. She had decided to spend the day in bed.

Joel was also in bed, for he was too stiff to move, and one leg was so swollen that he could not put it to the ground.

He was looking very woe-begone when Philadelphia went to see him, and asked immediately, "Does Grace want to marry that oaf?"

"I don't believe she's ever wanted anything else. And he isn't an oaf. He's young and raw, and he was reared in a hard school. All the same . . . "

"He's half a Martel and half a Tabor and I suppose that makes all the difference."

It struck Philadelphia that the boy had been able to face Laurence last night on something surprisingly close to equal terms. They spoke the same language, those two, and presumably it was the language of their common ancestry. But none of this would mean much to Grace.

"I think," she said, "that children who grow up in such places must set all their affections on each other. Coney isn't simply Grace's sweetheart, he's

307

her brother, friend, protector, all her kindred. I believe he has always taken care of her; he seems to have been totally undaunted by the terrors of the Charity Hospital. Unlike poor Grace." Philadelphia hesitated. It seemed unkind to taunt Joel in his present plight, but she could not resist one question.

"What made you embark on such an enterprise with so unlikely a partner? Some girls would have revelled in it, but Grace is a timid creature."

"I know," he said. "I must have been mad. The scheme came to me, all of a sudden, after I'd seen her for the first time, in an ice-cold room, ministering to a gaggle of orphans. I hadn't intended to cheat Mrs. Tabor, I wasn't looking for revenge at that moment either. I'd hoped to earn the reward. When I came to weigh up my plan, those reasons seemed good enough. But if you could have seen that beautiful girl, imprisoned in her mean clothes, in that barren room, with nothing to call her own, when so much money was going begging — maybe that's why I did it: to put such a jewel in the setting she deserved.

"She never enjoyed it," he continued after a minute, turning restlessly in the bed, and plucking at the crumpled edge of the sheet. "She always felt guilty and afraid. As you say, she had no stomach for the part, and I made matters worse for her. I wanted to marry her — to get hold of her dowry, that's what I told myself; I thought it a splendid solution to all my troubles. But when she refused me, made it plain she wanted nothing to do with me, I was angry, and I reminded her of the fate she would suffer if I gave her away. Oh God, how could I have been such a brute? When I saw her in the water yesterday, I felt as though I'd done that outrage to her myself."

"You saved her life," said Philadelphia.

"If I hadn't led her astray, she wouldn't have been in danger."

This was undoubtedly true. Then his remorse took a different turn.

"I was so impatient. She was too good, too innocent for me. If I'd used her more gently, she might have learnt to love me."

Philadelphia thought privately that Joel would never have stood a chance against

309

Coney, though there did not seem much purpose in arguing.

She did persuade Grace to say good-bye to her fellow-conspirator before leaving with Mrs. Iredale for Bristol.

"Must I, Del?" pleaded the girl, her blue eyes clouded with apprehension. "He frightens me."

"He couldn't frighten anyone at the moment, poor Joel. Besides, I think he wants to tell you he is sorry."

"You won't leave me alone with him?"

Philadelphia promised, and found herself, therefore, a most unwilling witness of this farewell scene. Grace stood just inside the door, giving Joel no help as he stumbled through his speech of contrition. She was a kind-hearted girl, and when she saw him looking so bruised and wretched she no longer felt hostile, but she hadn't got the words to separate the complicated emotions that were stirring under the surface of her mind. So she whispered a few unsatisfying phrases: that he mustn't take all the blame, truly there was no need, and escaped as fast as she could.

How unjust life is, thought Philadelphia. She has the empty prettiness of a doll, with no more wit and no more courage, yet she's got those two young men willing to go through fire for her. Even Laurence wasn't immune. He had spent very little time reproaching her after she was found out; he'd been too busy making plans to save her from the consequences of her own folly.

Philadelphia went into her bedchamber and stood gazing out of the window. Presently Coney and Grace appeared in the garden below, walking silently together, hand in hand. At the sight of them, her bitterness melted. Grace might not be able to say anything very profound, but there was no doubt that some of her feelings ran deep, especially her love for Coney. Eventually she would give him everything most men asked for in a wife. The qualities she lacked, such as an independent spirit or an educated mind, were an uncomfortable sort of dowry.

In the meantime, they had to face another parting: two children who had always been at the mercy of other people's arbitrary demands. That last day, as they wandered over the dewy grass, Philadelphia's heart ached for them. Yet she knew that they were safer than they had ever been. They had friends on their side now, and everything to look forward to. A great deal more to look forward to, for instance, than she had. Or poor Joel, who was lying on his back, staring into the dark hood of the curtains and wondering what was to become of him.

Joel tried to dismiss Grace from his mind by thinking about his own future. He wouldn't be prosecuted, that was one consolation, since Laurence had let Grace off scot free, and it would be impossible to bring a case against one of them without accusing the other. It was not surprising that Laurence wanted to spare Grace, she was so childish and ignorant that no one could have taken her for anything but a dupe. Joel did not expect such clemency for himself. He was a grown man who had known what he was doing, he had set out to defraud his former master's widow, he had abused a position of trust. Laurence had the power, not only to dismiss him, but to get him expelled from the Goldsmiths' Company, and then how would he contrive to live?

One other person was to escape prosecution, since Grace would not be there to give evidence, and that was Wacey. But the steward's star had waned; the villagers had been affronted by his latest witch-hunt, especially when his charges of necromancy had been answered in such a matter-of-fact way. He left Thurley two days later, with the air of a misunderstood minor prophet, and the village was a healthier place with out him. So that Laurence felt able to return to London, taking Coney, and leaving Philadelphia in charge of the household for as long as Mrs. Tabor and Joel needed to recuperate.

She spent a week there with these two gloomy companions. It might have been a good deal worse, if Mrs. Tabor had felt vengeful towards Joel, but she was too busy trying to clear up her own confusion of mind. The false Frances and her sponsor were easier to relinquish than the imaginary Frances who had never existed.

Gradually she became more resigned to the truth, and began to hanker for some of the small pleasures of the City. There was only one thing she dreaded about going home, and that was the prospect of the homilies she was going to get from her sister. Mrs. Beck had always said that it was a mistake to bring Grace Wilton from the Charity Hospital; events had proved her right, and nothing would induce her to hold her tongue.

27

ON the morning after their return to London, Hannah Beck arrived in Cheapside to perform the sisterly duty of pointing out to poor Alice where she had gone wrong.

"You would have been wiser to listen to those of us who have your true interests at heart," she announced, sitting bolt upright on the day-bed which occupied one corner of the great chamber.

It was not a setting that flattered her; she looked much too large and stiff on a seat that was meant for graceful reclining, and the pile of embroidered cushions, purple and red, clashed violently with her high complexion and brass-coloured hair.

"I told you all along that the girl was an imposter, didn't I, now?"

"Yes," whispered Mrs. Tabor, defeated and cowed.

"It stands to reason, you were not fit to conduct such a search, you were bound to be taken in. Your life has been so easy, John always shielded you from every care. Why, you didn't even know whether your precious grandchild was a boy or a girl," said Mrs. Beck in a jolly, rallying tone. "You must forgive me laughing, Alice, but you have been a great simpleton."

"Madam, I think I must tell you that it distresses Mrs. Tabor to talk of these matters," said Philadelphia in a low voice, trying to hide her indignation.

"I'm sure you prefer to think so, Mrs. Whitethorn. Better for you if the whole business was forgotten. You were very much to the fore in encouraging my sister to trust that jade and her paramour."

There was just enough truth in this to make Philadelphia feel uncomfortable. She was collecting her wits when Laurence came into the room with Edmund. Mrs. Beck greeted them complacently, and told Laurence that she knew he had no patience with people who were robbed through their own stupidity. What ever his faults, Laurence had always been courteous to his aunt, and Philadelphia hoped he might pour cold water on Mrs. Beck's pretensions, it was the sort of thing he could do extremely well. But Laurence answered at random and signalled a question to Edmund in some kind of dumbshow. Both young men seemed surprised and disconcerted at the sight of Mrs. Beck.

"Joel was not Grace's paramour," said Mrs. Tabor, pursuing the discussion at her own pace. "She was a good girl and would never have consented."

"My dear Alice, you are wilfully blinding yourself. Just as you did over Frances."

"For pity's sake, Hannah, must you reproach me with that, yet again? Haven't I suffered enough?"

"Mother, how can you be so heartless?" burst out Edmund.

His mother ignored him. "I wasn't reproaching you, Alice," she said in a slightly aggrieved tone. "The fact is, you're too innocent. You could never take the measure of a wicked, wayward fly-by-night like Frances . . . "

"She wasn't wicked and wayward! Or if she was, you've no right to say so to me. Can't you understand? each time you tell me how foolish I've been, I

317

feel guilty, and each time you tell me how wicked she was, I feel miserable. And what good does it all do, when she's been dead fifteen years? I wish you would leave me alone!"

"There's no need to shout at me," said Mrs. Beck, affronted. "You know very well that anything I say is meant for your own good."

"And you are tireless in searching out other people's good, aren't you, Mother?" burst out Edmund.

"I want no impudence from you, Edmund. Lucky for you your father didn't hear you!" His mother looked him over carefully, and asked why he was wearing his best doublet on a working day? That milaine velvet had cost too much to be wasted on the shop; he ought to take more care of his new clothes, hadn't she always told him that he must overcome his sinful extravagance?

Edmund confronted her, hot with mortification. He had a quiet, pleasant manner, an ineffectual charm, and a certain air of the scholar he would have liked to be. His parents — at any rate, his mother — had no use for book-learning, so he had been apprenticed to John Tabor and hammered into the semblance of a goldsmith. He had never been much of a craftsman, he hadn't got the right sort of hands. He was accustomed, like all Mrs. Beck's children, to the ignominy of being asked in public why he was wearing his best doublet.

He answered, with unusual truculence, "I've been to a wedding."

A wedding, thought Philadelphia. A painful suspicion edged into her mind, as she observed that Laurence was also dressed with particular elegance. Quilted chestnut satin, laced with gold thread — it was good enough for a bridegroom. And Edmund was Judith's brother.

"Don't you want to hear about the wedding, Mother?" continued Edmund. "My sister Judith was married two hours ago to Walter Brand."

"To Walter Brand!" repeated Philadelphia, forgetting that she was not a member of the family and it was nothing to do with her. Luckily no one seemed to notice.

Mrs. Tabor blew her nose and gazed

319

bemusedly at Edmund over the edge of her handkerchief.

Mrs. Beck was incredulous. "What kind of jest is this? I've no patience with you when you start talking nonsense . . . It is nonsense, isn't it?" She appealed to Laurence, suddenly apprehensive.

"It's perfectly true, madam. They were married this morning at St. Dunstan's Church."

"But why? What reason had they for such unseemly haste and secrecy?" A fearful possibly leapt to the eye. "You don't mean to tell me that my Judith allowed herself to be led astray? In the summer when we were at Thurley? I can't believe it!"

"I don't mean to tell you any such thing," said Laurence briskly. "Brand married her because he loves her, and not out of necessity."

And dear Judith is as pure as driven snow, thought Philadelphia. That was a foregone conclusion. She did not wish the girl any harm, but it would have been pleasant to find that one of Mrs. Beck's children was capable of error. As it was, they were faced with another example of natural injustice. Frances Tabor's escapade had ended in tragedy. But when one of Mrs. Beck's precious daughters ran away with a lover, he immediately married her and raised her to a position of dignity and consequence. Though it certainly did seem odd, on thinking it over, that such an acceptable match should have been hustled through in a furtive way which suggested scandal where no scandal existed.

Mrs. Beck evidently though this too. "I don't understand why they did it," she kept saying.

"Then I'll tell you, Mother," said Edmund in a hard, unnatural voice. "They did it because you were forever coming between them . . . "

"Coming between them? What wild talk is this? I never . . . "

"Judith said you were always there at her elbow, directing every movement she made, reproving all her actions, interpreting her thoughts, answering questions for her before she could get a word in edgeways. She says she became so stupid and anxious that she could take no pleasure in Brand's company, so that he might soon have fallen out of love with her — and besides, it made him angry to see a girl so timorous in the presence of her mother, and that caused a dissension between them. So in the end she asked him to marry her privately and take her out of your reach. And I don't blame her."

"You're mad! I won't listen . . . "

"Yes, you will." Edmund raised his voice. "It's time someone told you how much harm you do. Judith is only one of your victims. You forced me to become a goldsmith's apprentice, when I wanted to stay at school and go on to the university — and the result is I'm a bad craftsman instead of a passable scholar. You nagged my brother Tom into marrying a rich wife who makes him miserable; you drove a wedge between Joan and her husband, so that they quarrel every time you visit them. You've made my father a figure of contempt in his own shop, and you continually mortify my aunt by dwelling on troubles that are nearly twenty years old. You can never leave well alone. Or ill alone, come to that. Most people know their own business best, and even when they don't, they would rather make their own mistakes than dwindle into puppets, dragged this way and that by the strings of your everlasting interference!"

She stared at them all for an instant after he had stopped; they could hardly recognise the gentle, diffident, amenable Edmund through this impassioned bitterness. He turned and went out of the room; they could hear him running down the stairs in the silence that followed.

Mrs. Beck had not spoken. She was breathing heavily and she had gone strangely pale, except for the blotched veins high on her cheeks, which were almost purple. Slowly the tears began to slide out of her eyes, noiseless and unchecked, as though she was not aware of them.

"How could he be so cruel?" she said at last. "My dear Edmund, that was always my favourite. And Judith — to run away because — how could she say that I was preventing her happiness? I wanted her to find a bridegroom who was worthy of her, I wanted to help her. I wanted to help them all."

"That's what most mothers want,"

said Mrs. Tabor. "Now perhaps you see how easy it is to mismanage a beloved child."

It was her moment of triumph, of justification. She had no talent for revenge, however, and gave up her advantage in immediate compassion.

"Come, my dear Hannah — come into my chamber, and you shall bathe your eyes, and take a draught of my special cordial to revive you. Edmund didn't mean what he said. These children never know how much they can hurt us."

With a curious reversal of their usual roles, she led her sister away, leaving Philadelphia alone with Laurence.

She gazed at him speechless after the hammer-blows of so many different surprises. One fact dominated the rest. There was no longer any question of his marrying Judith. He did not look as though he minded; had he ever expected to marry her?

"How long have you known?" she asked. "About Mr. Brand and Judith — were you in their confidence?"

"Yes, I've known since the spring, ever since he first came here when I was painting her portrait and fell instantly in love with her. That's why I brought him to Thurley; I shouldn't otherwise have invited him into such a family party. It must have seemed strange to you; both Walter and I were all for letting you know how matters stood. But Judith did not wish it. She is a little afraid of you."

"Afraid of me! Good heavens, why?"

"I dare say it was all part of the humility that has been so driven into her by her mother. You belong to the same world as Walter Brand, you understand the mysteries of life on a gentleman's country estate, besides being so fearless in the saddle and an excellent musician, and the poor girl was sure you must despise her."

"I am sorry if I ever gave her cause to think so," said Philadelphia uncomfortably.

"I am sure you never did. But those two had got themselves into such a tangle; they could hardly ever be alone together, and when they were, Walter kept trying to stiffen her resolution against her mother. He could not bear to see her being so browbeaten, and it took him some time to discover that poor Judith could not overcome the dependency of a lifetime as though she was casting off an old cloak. Do you remember our last ride together — the day your horse lost a shoe?"

"Yes." (So that was why he had followed her, when she rode off by herself; to give the lovers a chance of being alone.)

"When they rejoined us, outside that wood, I could have murdered them both. But I could see at once that something was wrong; that was why I left you in such a cavalier fashion, and rode ahead with Judith. I tell you, I got heartily sick of playing both Cupid and Mercury for the pair of them, at Thurley and then here in London. In the end they decided to marry in secret and tell her mother afterwards, and I admit I encouraged them. I wouldn't have done so if I hadn't felt certain that Walter would make her a very good husband, besides being an excellent match."

"No. I mean, yes," murmured Philadelphia automatically.

How stupid she had been, that afternoon when she thought that Judith's and

Brand's glum faces were hostile with disapproval; they must have been too wretched, poor creatures, to notice anyone else's follies. Laurence's preoccupation with Judith, even that scrap of talk Mrs. Tabor had overheard next day in the gallery — all this took on a new aspect. But what had he meant, just now, when he said he could have murdered them both, outside the wood?

She was wondering how she could ask, when the door opened, and Joel looked in, shied like a nervous horse, and made to withdraw.

"Are you looking for me?" asked Laurence.

"Yes, but it doesn't signify. I'll come back later."

Having nerved himself to the point of seeking an interview with Laurence, he was ready to clutch at any excuse for putting it off.

"I'll leave you," Philadelphia said, as Joel hovered unhappily.

"I'd prefer you to stay, Mrs. Whitethorn. If you please. I want a witness of what I am going to say to Joel."

Philadelphia stayed. She was almost

sure Joel did not want a witness, but she could not help being curious, and perhaps she could help in some way, by pouring oil on troubled waters. (She hoped she wasn't getting like Mrs. Beck.)

"Sit down, Joel," said Laurence. "We've got a good deal to talk about, one way and another. You can begin."

"I?" said Joel, taken aback.

"Well, you came up here to find me, didn't you?"

"Oh. Yes. To — to say I'm sorry. For the distress I've caused Mrs. Tabor; it was a cruel thing to do, I didn't entirely perceive at the time — but that's no excuse. And protests of contrition sound rather thin, don't they? Once one has been found out."

"Why did you do it?"

"You know very well why I did it," said Joel, raising his head a little and looking directly at Laurence. "For the money. Are you going to get me turned out of the Company?"

"What do you expect me to do?"

"Well, you can't prosecute me, because you let Grace go — and that was an act of mercy that it's not my place to

328

thank you for. You could simply send me packing, without informing the Company what's happened, but why should you spare me? I've robbed your family, which is as bad as stealing from the shop, and for that they can certainly break me. I should be left with no trade and no means of earning my living. I deserve no better, and I shouldn't have the impudence to complain, but I wanted to ask you, sir, not to visit my sins on my father and Sam. I don't believe you would let innocent people suffer — I should be very grateful if you would tell me whether you mean to go on employing them."

The bleak voice died away. Joel sat hunched on his stool, nervously smoothing the wrinkles out of his sleeve.

"Make your mind easy," said Laurence. "I should not think of persecuting either your father or Sam. It's what I am to do with you that concerns me. You've placed me in a damnable predicament."

"I have?" said Joel, startled.

Philadelphia remembered Laurence saying something of the sort to her and

Bess Iredale in the gallery at Thurley, just before they were interrupted by the cries from the lake. It was extremely tantalising, his habit of making cryptic remarks.

"What possessed you, to get embroiled in such a harebrained scheme?" he demanded. "I should have thought there were easier ways of making money. You set out to look for my cousin — I credit you with that, for you got as far as the Charity Hospital — yet you never managed to find out that the child you were following was a boy. You're not the most skilful of intriguers, are you?"

It was a sign of poor Joel's change of heart that he didn't bristle up arrogantly at this derision, but merely said, "I went to Cobchurch and the cottagers I spoke to had seen the child simply as a babe in arms; they sent me directly to the Southwark tavern. The people there told me a story that they'd inherited when they bought the place; they didn't know for certain whether the abandoned child was a boy or a girl . . . I never doubted that your aunt knew the sex of her own grandchild — though I ought to have done, now I come to think of it, for I'd heard the contents of Mrs. Iredale's letter."

"So had I," remarked Philadelphia. "I was as dull as you, and Mr. Tabor can afford to scoff at us both."

Laurence had the grace to say, "I was forewarned; I already believed the child to be a boy. But I suppose it has now dawned on you, Joel, that if you'd asked the right questions, the answers would have led you straight to Coney Martel and you'd have earned your reward honestly instead of sinking to the level of a common thief."

"Coney wouldn't have wanted to come to Goldsmiths' Row," said Philadelphia, seeing that Joel looked too wretched to speak.

"What of it?" replied Laurence. "My aunt had promised to reward the person who found her grandchild, and she would have kept her word. However, that's neither here nor there." He turned back to Joel. "Having failed to find a girl called Frances Perry, you conceived the notion of putting a deputy in her place?"

"I'd seen Grace and she was so pretty;

I thought Mrs. Tabor would sooner have her than no one."

"You had no compunction in cheating her, I suppose. An unprotected woman who had always been kind to you?"

Joel did not answer.

"Well?" prompted Laurence.

"What do you want me to say. Don't you think I'm ashamed of what I've done?"

"I thought you might suggest that your family were entitled to a settlement from my uncle's estate."

"Oh no!" said Joel. "I swore to myself that I wouldn't bring that up. It's no proper defence, and in any case, why should you believe that your uncle owed us anything?"

"I believe it because he told me so."

Joel jerked upright. "He did what?"

"He left a letter for me with his attorney, in which he said that he had a moral obligation to take your father into partnership, as he had promised and in recognition of many years' hard work. He had not done so because he knew that your father's mind was rigidly set in the past, and if he was given too much say in the management of the shop, he would lose money hand over fist. My uncle was set in his ways also, but he knew what to buy and sell, for all that. He was afraid that Mr. Zachary would not be so successful."

"It's true," said Joel sadly. He had made no attempt to deny these strictures. "My father is no longer fit to take complete charge. Perhaps he never was. But why couldn't your uncle have redeemed his promise by giving him a lump sum?"

"Because he had a better idea. He suggested that I should take you into partnership instead. He wrote that it would not seem strange if I preferred to take a partner younger than myself. He thought you and I should discuss the matter and then put it to your father with as much diplomacy as we could manage."

"Then why didn't you — Oh!"

"Yes," said Laurence, surveying him ironically. "By the time I read that letter, I knew that my intended partner was engaged in the criminal enterprise of defrauding my uncle's widow out of a large sum of money."

"Oh, God," said Joel, with a sort of groan, "why did I have to be such a fool?"

There was a short interval, during which Philadelphia felt extremely sorry for him, and Laurence took off a ring he always wore and began absently polishing the engraved crystal with his thumb.

Presently he said, "What's past is over and done with. Can you think of any overwhelming reason why we should not still enter into this partnership?"

"You cannot mean that!" said Joel, staring. "You'd never trust me."

"I don't think you'd try to cheat me. Why should you? We could prosper only if we worked in harmony, and I'm sure you have the wit to see that."

"Even so, I no longer have any claim on you . . . "

"You seem determined to spoil your own chances. Don't you want to stay here?"

"You must know very well that I do. After watching you at work these last few months, there's nothing I should like better — the fact is, I've often wanted to ask if I could try my hand at fashioning some of those new jewels, but I was afraid you'd refuse. You had Ralph and the boys at your beck and call, but I was always excluded and my conscience told me why."

"Well, what do you think my conscience was doing? I knew I ought to tell you what was in my uncle's letter; I also knew that you'd taken the law into your own hands and that I had got to stop you fleecing my aunt. What sort of friendship could I offer you in those circumstances? I kept hoping that either you or Grace might come out with the truth of your own accord. I certainly had no other reason for leaving you out in the cold. Just the contrary."

Joel said uncertainly, "You are very generous."

"Not entirely. Don't let yourself feel too grateful. Too heavy a burden of gratitude on one side is fatal to any fraternal endeavour. I think we each have a great deal to give the other. I need you here; unless you stay, I shall have to abandon my painting in order to work as a silversmith. You know yourself that the forging and casting of silver plate will always provide the solid foundation of our livelihood. By making jewelled ornaments we can earn a useful profit and a certain measure of fame. But limning — that's very highly thought of, an occupation worthy of a gentleman; unfortunately, like most of the occupations of the gentry, it's remarkably ill-paid. Look at Nick Hilliard — the Queen's limner, with a monopoly for painting her miniatures, and he's never out of debt. I don't want to travel the road. Yet how can I paint and keep shop at the same time, unless I take a partner who's fit to manage the day-to-day work on his own? Your father, as we've said, is too old. Edmund hasn't the skill. Ralph's a better workman than I shall ever be, but he hasn't the schooling or the judgment. I'd never find a craftsman of your quality who was free to take your place — but if you remain as our chief silversmith, while I continue as a painter, then together we can devise such jewels as no one in London has ever seen or dreamed of. You'd have to submit a masterpiece at Goldsmiths' Hall before I could take you into partnership, but you

336

needn't lose any sleep over that. So what do you say? No, don't tell me now. Go away and think it over."

Joel got up, like an obedient child. Philadelphia saw that he was completely dazed by the unexpected prospect before him. She thought he must have been secretly longing to escape from his false position ever since he discovered what sort of a goldsmith Laurence really was. He had certainly made none of his usual aggressive remarks or self-justifying excuses; she could not decide whether this was due to his respect for Laurence or to the softening influence of his unrequited love for Grace. Either way, he had done himself a good turn.

He paused in the doorway, a conflict of emotions in his handsome and sometimes rather sulky face. "I can't thank you enough — Oh! I'm not allowed to be grateful! Very well, sir. I'll go."

When the door was safely shut behind him, Laurence said: "Heaven be praised that he was able to forgive me for forgiving him. I thought I might have trouble with his confounded pride, but

I took him by surprise. I hope you approve?"

"Yes, indeed," said Philadelphia, rather astonished to be asked. "I think you have been very generous — if I'm allowed to say so with impunity."

"You are allowed to say anything you choose."

"In that case, I also think it was a little hard on Joel to have his misdeeds dealt with, however mercifully, in front of a third person, and woman into the bargain. You said you wanted a witness, but I can't see why."

"I would like you to understand all my plans regarding the shop."

"Would you?" she thought this over. "So that I can explain matters to your aunt?"

"It has nothing whatever to do with my aunt!"

"No, I suppose not. She has her jointure, hasn't she?"

Laurence seemed rather put out, and made some rambling remarks about merchants' wives and daughters often knowing a good deal about their families' commercial dealings; he thought it was right that they should.

"I've no doubt of it," agreed Philadelphia, her mind still dwelling on his aunt. "Mrs. Tabor might have been happier with more to occupy her mind."

Laurence looked at her with an expression that was almost dislike, and asked, "Do you always make matters so difficult? Acting as though you'd never had an offer of marriage before?"

"I never have," said Philadelphia, complete frankness being bounced out of her unawares. "Is — is that what you're doing?"

"Yes, it is, and a proper botch I'm making of it," he replied crossly. Something odd seemed to strike him. He paused, "Have you always managed to silence your suitors before they came to the point? You don't mean to live and die a virgin, I hope?"

"I thought I might have to." She had not yet recovered her natural defences of discretion and reserve. "How many suitors do you think I've had?"

"How can I tell? I know you frightened away several of my friends, and at times you've frightened me. The story's got

339

around that you would never stoop to marry a shopkeeper — but in that case why did you come here at all? A pretty girl with a sufficient dowry can always find a husband of her own station."

"Pretty!" she repeated. "You can spare your breath, I don't have to be flattered into complaisance. If you think the blood of my forefathers is a fair exchange for all you have to offer, we may as well be honest. You can't pretend to admire my — my deformity."

"What the devil are you talking about?"

"Surely you of all men, a portrait-painter, must find it so hideous, even repulsive . . . "

She could not go on, but sat staring in front of her, clenching and unclenching her hands in her lap.

"Philadelphia," said Laurence in a voice of incredulity, "are you performing this tragedy because you've got a few pock-marks on your forehead?"

Philadelphia brust into tears.

He crossed the room and sat down beside her on the day-bed, taking hold of both her hands.

"Listen, my dear. You're not suffering from any grave disfigurement. Everyone can see you've had smallpox, which is neither here nor there, except that you won't catch it again. I assure you that those scars don't matter. Your skin has the texture of velvet and the bones beneath are incomparably fine — that's what a painter looks for, didn't you know? As for a lover, that's different again. No man chooses his mistress simply by looking at her face, didn't you know that either?"

Philadelphia had stopped crying; she gazed at him in speechless hope and wonder. He took her in his arms and kissed her gently on the forehead. He might have been working a charm, in fact the result was equally magical. The blotched and puckered skin remained, but not the far more distorting ravages that were always present in her mind's eye. They vanished instantly, never to return.

Then he kissed her mouth, and she lay back among the cushions of the day-bed; there was a long time while neither of them spoke, until Laurence remarked,

"This is better than that confounded tree-stump."

"Our last afternoon at Thurley?" her voice was still husky and uneven. "You weren't preparing to speak of marriage, then?"

"Yes, I was. But you were so fierce, I never plucked up the courage."

"Good heavens, I thought . . . "

"I expect you thought I was a terrible coxcomb, eaten up with my own conceit," he said ruefully. "It's always so when I feel despised and mortified. I never get any pity, because I immediately become excessively vainglorious and start sharpening my wits on everyone within reach. That's what happened when I first arrived home."

"Oh, poor Laurence," she said, paying off all her arrears of compassion. "You did seem to be in a vainglorious mood that day. You assured me that you painted endless portraits of yourself to hand out to your doting admirers."

"Did I? What a stupid clown I am. I tell you what, my girl: as soon as we're married I'll give you a likeness of myself that you'll carry next to your heart and treasure more than all you possess. And that will be a work of singular perfection."

"Very well," she said smiling. "And how many of these works of singular perfection am I to cherish?"

"Half a dozen at least."

"I thank you, sir. You mean to be a prodigal giver. Are there to be any daughters among the miniature goldsmiths?"

"I'd like to call our eldest daughter Frances, to please my aunt," he said, becoming serious. "Would you be willing, sweetheart, for her to continue living with us? She is so attached to you already."

"Of course she must stay here," said Philadelphia warmly. It dawned on her that their children would provide the perfect solace for Mrs. Tabor's loneliness and disappointments.

"What a kind girl you are," said Laurence in a loving voice.

She leant against his shoulder, learning to accept the amazing happiness that had swept over her like a tidal wave. It was surprisingly easy to believe that he loved her, once she had grasped the fact that he did not mind about the scars. Had she been behaving like a mad creature all these years, driving away possible husbands not by her looks, but with her tongue? If so, she was glad. Suppose she had married some dull squire in Gloucestershire, she would never have come to Goldsmiths' Row. She had never seen a man who could hold a candle to Laurence.

Once she'd come to London, however, the fault wasn't all on her side.

"I'm sorry I seem so proud to the people here," she said, "but it's not easy for a woman to know how far she should encourage a man unless he is presented to her as a possible suitor. Your uncle was supposed to find an acceptable match for me, that's what he promised my brother, but I don't believe he ever tried to."

"I'm afraid my uncle failed in his duty towards you. He had his reasons, however."

"Laurence! Do you mean that I was included in his legacy to you, along with Joel? One partner for your shop and another for your bed?"

"Yes, and a delightful windfall I found you, both determined to be my sworn enemies. Now, love, there's no use taking umbrage. You can't back out now, just to spite my uncle's ghost."

"Who said I was backing out? I shall simply demand the right to abuse him as much as I please. He was an abominable old despot. All the troubles we've had in the last six months were largely of his making. Your having to go abroad in the first place, and coming back as though you were a stranger. His treatment of the Downes family, which had such a ruinous effect on Joel. And his unkindness to your poor aunt, not allowing her any news of her grandchild, so that she's lived all these years in a dream. And worst of all, failing to make provision for his daughter's child. Did he mention either of them in his letter?"

"I think he had blotted the matter from his mind. Frances has been dead so many years, and as for the boy, I believe the old man did take steps to see that he was properly cared for. I think someone must have given Cicely some money, for she managed to find a husband who was willing to accept the baby as well, and she herself was neither young nor handsome. Francis was happy as a small child, he says both the Perrys were very good to him. It was the misfortune of their dying on the same day, and in a strange place, that landed him in the Charity Hospital. Not the act that he was born out of wedlock."

"That's true," said Philadelphia reluctantly. She did not like to admit anything that tended to exonerate John Tabor. "I suppose you are certain this time that you've got the rightful claimant?"

"If I hadn't been convinced that evening at Thurley, I should be now. I've been shown some additional evidence."

"Where? At the Charity Hospital?"

"By Coney himself. When we came back to London, I went with him to his lodging, to make his peace with the old Dutchman, who thought, of course, that he'd run away. He was soon satisfied, however, and we had a long conference. He's an excellent fellow, he must have been a stone-carver of high standing in his own country, and now I've seen his work in the church across the street, I feel sure Coney could have no better master. While I was there, the boy showed me a bird he'd carved out of a broken piece of alabaster, and also some drawings he'd made, simply as an exercise. He had designed a monumental tomb supposed to contain the body of some famous mariner. The drawings were marvellously exact, and so was his alabaster cockerel. There's no doubt at all that he's inherited the family touch."

"How strange it is, the way these gifts are transmitted in the blood. Are you sorry that he'll never be a goldsmith?"

"A little. I should have liked to have him as my pupil. When you are a young craftsman, there are so many images spinning in your brain that you can hardly wait to get them out. In time you recognise your own limitations, and it's then you begin to think of teaching someone who will have the ability to go on where you left off. I should have liked to see Coney turn his particular images into silver and gold; after all, it's the stiff we Tabors have worked for three hundred years. But this is a small matter. Coney has no regrets, I fancy he considers the making of jewellery a trivial pastime; cutting stone is the proper occupation for a man. And I've no doubt he'll do it very well. He won't make a fortune, but he should earn a fair living, especially if I can introduce him to the right patrons when he's ready to set up on his own. I may also induce him to accept some money from the family, so that he won't have to wait too long before marrying Grace. If they are still set on marriage."

"They will be," said Philadelphia.

"Yes, I think so too."

They drifted into a companionable silence, Philadelphia thought over what he had been saying. She had caught in his voice that elusive note in which a countryman might speak of the land. Laurence felt the same mixture of emotions about the practice of his craft, pride and humility, hard, practical sense, and sheer delight. He was the master and also the servant of the inanimate metal, the innocent parchment. On them he was compelled to make visible the mysterious power that God had put into his head and into his hands. And her sons would take after him.

The sunlight poured across the floor in little segments shaped like the leaded window-panes. They could hear the creak of coaches and wagons trundling over the cobbles, the monotonous yet haunting lilt of the street-criers, the constant tread of footsteps in the street, as the people passed and paused and looked up at the ten tall houses in Goldsmiths' Row.

THE END

THE WILDERNESS WALK
Sheila Bishop

Stifling unpleasant memories of a misbegotten romance in Cleave with Lord Francis Aubrey, Lavinia goes on holiday there with her sister. The two women are thrust into a romantic intrigue involving none other than Lord Francis.

THE RELUCTANT GUEST
Rosalind Brett

Ann Calvert went to spend a month on a South African farm with Theo Borland and his sister. They both proved to be different from her first idea of them, and there was Storr Peterson — the most disturbing man she had ever met.

ONE ENCHANTED SUMMER
Anne Tedlock Brooks

A tale of mystery and romance and a girl who found both during one enchanted summer.

CLOUD OVER MALVERTON
Nancy Buckingham

Dulcie soon realises that something is seriously wrong at Malverton, and when violence strikes she is horrified to find herself under suspicion of murder.

AFTER THOUGHTS
Max Bygraves

The Cockney entertainer tells stories of his East End childhood, of his RAF days, and his post-war showbusiness successes and friendships with fellow comedians.

MOONLIGHT
AND MARCH ROSES
D. Y. Cameron

Lynn's search to trace a missing girl takes her to Spain, where she meets Clive Hendon. While untangling the situation, she untangles her emotions and decides on her own future.

NURSE ALICE IN LOVE
Theresa Charles

Accepting the post of nurse to little Fernie Sherrod, Alice Everton could not guess at the romance, suspense and danger which lay ahead at the Sherrod's isolated estate.

POIROT INVESTIGATES
Agatha Christie

Two things bind these eleven stories together — the brilliance and uncanny skill of the diminutive Belgian detective, and the stupidity of his Watson-like partner, Captain Hastings.

LET LOOSE THE TIGERS
Josephine Cox

Queenie promised to find the long-lost son of the frail, elderly murderess, Hannah Jason. But her enquiries threatened to unlock the cage where crucial secrets had long been held captive.

THE TWILIGHT MAN
Frank Gruber

Jim Rand lives alone in the California desert awaiting death. Into his hermit existence comes a teenage girl who blows both his past and his brief future wide open.

DOG IN THE DARK
Gerald Hammond

Jim Cunningham breeds and trains gun dogs, and his antagonism towards the devotees of show spaniels earns him many enemies. So when one of them is found murdered, the police are on his doorstep within hours.

THE RED KNIGHT
Geoffrey Moxon

When he finds himself a pawn on the chessboard of international espionage with his family in constant danger, Guy Trent becomes embroiled in moves and countermoves which may mean life or death for Western scientists.

TIGER TIGER
Frank Ryan

A young man involved in drugs is found murdered. This is the first event which will draw Detective Inspector Sandy Woodings into a whirlpool of murder and deceit.

CAROLINE MINUSCULE
Andrew Taylor

Caroline Minuscule, a medieval script, is the first clue to the whereabouts of a cache of diamonds. The search becomes a deadly kind of fairy story in which several murders have an other-worldly quality.

LONG CHAIN OF DEATH
Sarah Wolf

During the Second World War four American teenagers from the same town join the Army together. Forty-two years later, the son of one of the soldiers realises that someone is systematically wiping out the families of the four men.

THE LISTERDALE MYSTERY
Agatha Christie

Twelve short stories ranging from the light-hearted to the macabre, diverse mysteries ingeniously and plausibly contrived and convincingly unravelled.

TO BE LOVED
Lynne Collins

Andrew married the woman he had always loved despite the knowledge that Sarah married him for reasons of her own. So much heartache could have been avoided if only he had known how vital it was to be loved.

ACCUSED NURSE
Jane Converse

Paula found herself accused of a crime which could cost her her job, her nurse's reputation, and even the man she loved, unless the truth came to light.

A GREAT DELIVERANCE
Elizabeth George

Into the web of old houses and secrets of Keldale Valley comes Scotland Yard Inspector Thomas Lynley and his assistant to solve a particularly savage murder.

'E' IS FOR EVIDENCE
Sue Grafton

Kinsey Millhone was bogged down on a warehouse fire claim. It came as something of a shock when she was accused of being on the take. She'd been set up. Now she had a new client — herself.

A FAMILY OUTING IN AFRICA
Charles Hampton and Janie Hampton

A tale of a young family's journey through Central Africa by bus, train, river boat, lorry, wooden bicycle and foot.

THE PLEASURES OF AGE
Robert Morley

The author, British stage and screen star, now eighty, is enjoying the pleasures of age. He has drawn on his experiences to write this witty, entertaining and informative book.

THE VINEGAR SEED
Maureen Peters

The first book in a trilogy which follows the exploits of two sisters who leave Ireland in 1861 to seek their fortune in England.

A VERY PAROCHIAL MURDER
John Wainwright

A mugging in the genteel seaside town turned to murder when the victim died. Then the body of a young tearaway is washed ashore and Detective Inspector Lyle is determined that a second killing will not go unpunished.

DEATH ON A HOT SUMMER NIGHT
Anne Infante

Micky Douglas is either accident-prone or someone is trying to kill him. He finds himself caught in a desperate race to save his ex-wife and others from a ruthless gang.

HOLD DOWN A SHADOW
Geoffrey Jenkins

Maluti Rider, with the help of four of the world's most wanted men, is determined to destroy the Katse Dam and release a killer flood.

THAT NICE MISS SMITH
Nigel Morland

A reconstruction and reassessment of the trial in 1857 of Madeleine Smith, who was acquitted by a verdict of Not Proven of poisoning her lover, Emile L'Angelier.

SEASONS OF MY LIFE
Hannah Hauxwell
and Barry Cockcroft

The story of Hannah Hauxwell's struggle to survive on a desolate farm in the Yorkshire Dales with little money, no electricity and no running water.

TAKING OVER
Shirley Lowe and Angela Ince

A witty insight into what happens when women take over in the boardroom and their husbands take over chores, children and chickenpox.

AFTER MIDNIGHT STORIES,
The Fourth Book Of

A collection of sixteen of the best of today's ghost stories, all different in style and approach but all combining to give the reader that special midnight shiver.

DEATH TRAIN
Robert Byrne

The tale of a freight train out of control and leaking a paralytic nerve gas that turns America's West into a scene of chemical catastrophe in which whole towns are rendered helpless.

THE ADVENTURE OF THE CHRISTMAS PUDDING
Agatha Christie

In the introduction to this short story collection the author wrote "This book of Christmas fare may be described as 'The Chef's Selection'. I am the Chef!"

RETURN TO BALANDRA
Grace Driver

Returning to her Caribbean island home, Suzanne looks forward to being with her parents again, but most of all she longs to see Wim van Branden, a coffee planter she has known all her life.

SKINWALKERS
Tony Hillerman

The peace of the land between the sacred mountains is shattered by three murders. Is a 'skinwalker', one who has rejected the harmony of the Navajo way, the murderer?

A PARTICULAR PLACE
Mary Hocking

How is Michael Hoath, newly arrived vicar of St. Hilary's, to meet the demands of his flock and his strained marriage? Further complications follow when he falls hopelessly in love with a married parishioner.

A MATTER OF MISCHIEF
Evelyn Hood

A saga of the weaving folk in 18th century Scotland. Physician Gavin Knox was desperately seeking a cure for the pox that ravaged the slums of Glasgow and Paisley, but his adored wife, Margaret, stood in the way.